Reunion in Saltwater Beach

JULIE CAROBINI

DOLPHIN GATE BOOKS

To Dancer (woof) ...
and the pups we've loved before.

Chapter One

"**M**y brother's here."

Addi didn't have to ask Lily which brother she was referring to. Her friend had four of them—including a set of twins—and though they would all be here today on this sad occasion of their mother's memorial, Addi had mainly been close to one of them when they were kids: Jax.

"Look," Lily said, handing her a stack of napkins to put on the table, "you don't have to engage him. I'll inform Jax that you're working for me today and you are off limits."

Addi took a quick intake of breath. "Don't say that. Our friendship was a long time ago–"

"Twelve years."

"Yes. Besides, I'm not that girl anymore—"

Lily snorted and kept moving, placing a stack of clear plastic cups on the table.

"I'm serious, Lily!" Addi forced her shoulders down, calming herself. "Shush now. I've made my life here in Salt-water Beach, for better or worse, and that's not going to

1

change. And Jax is a grown man with a career in the city that keeps him busy—"

"Too busy, if you ask me."

"Right. Busy twenty-four-seven, from what you've said. And anyway, we haven't spoken in so many years. It wouldn't even matter if he knew that I had a little thing for him back then. That's long over now."

"I sure hope so. I love my brother, but he can be a big flirt sometimes. He's broken his share of hearts, and the last thing I need him to do is swoop in and steal my best friend right from under me."

Addi shook her head. "Lily—that's not about to happen."

"You know what? When he gets here, I'm going to point you out to him and tell him to keep his filthy paws off—"

"Don't you dare." Addi attempted to keep a silly smile on her face, but there were things Lily didn't know about what happened that last summer Jax was here, and she wanted to keep it that way. No sense bringing up something that, even now, could get ugly.

"Fine. I could never really picture you two together anyway." Lily stopped, probably noticing the expression on Addi's face. "Oops. Sorry if that sounded harsh. I really do have trouble reading people sometimes."

"It's forgotten. Really."

Lily paused. "Listen, you and I only reconnected a short time ago, and I appreciate your friendship. I don't want to lose that. Promise me you won't blame me for my brother's attitude."

"Of course, I would never." Addi and Lily knew each other growing up, but weren't particularly close. They hadn't seen each other much over the years, but reacquainted two years ago when they were both ranting about the truly horrible coffee at

The Coffee Hole in downtown Saltwater Beach. They both agreed that if it weren't for the comfy couches and decent Wi-Fi, the place near a quiet swath of the California coast would be out of business for sure.

Lily exhaled. "It's been a long few months ..."

When her voice trailed off, Addi reached out and patted Lily's arm. She'd been through so much with her mother's illness and subsequent passing. The last thing Addi wanted to do was to make Lily more harried than usual. "I know, I know."

"I just want you to find the happiness you deserve, Addi. You know I love my big brother, but sometimes I want to smack him in the face." Lily sniffled, no doubt holding back built-up tears. "You need someone in your life who, finally, will be there for *you*. Sadly, Jax could never be that guy."

Lily gave her a quick side hug and turned to finish setting up the long serving table.

Sudden tears pricked the backs of Addi's eyes too. Yes, she had been hung up on Jax once, and looking back, Addi knew she had felt that way for most of her life. Not that he had ever noticed. She had tried to tell him that night ... well, the night that everything had changed, and for a moment beneath those stars in that big old beach sky, she thought he knew.

By the next day, though, she found herself scrambling to erase the moment, at least, from her own heart. For the most part, she had managed to do just that.

Addi turned back to her work, laying out napkins as methodically as an accountant populating a spreadsheet, but still reliving the past in her own mind. She needed to face the past once and for all. It was the only way she could truly move on.

"There he is."

She jerked her head up from her musings to see Lily making her way over to the entrance of this large and hollow room where the memorial would be held. Her heart thudded against her chest. The last thing she wanted to do today, on this solemn occasion, was to redirect the attention to her.

Her gaze caught Jax entering his mother's place. He pulled Lily into an embrace, holding her to him for several seconds. Addi had never had a sibling of her own and wondered what it would be like to have someone share some of her family's burdens.

Jax towered over his sister, as he always had, yet his arms had filled out over the years, muscles now in places where they hadn't been previously. He looked strong. And commanding. Addi sensed a shift in the home at his arrival, as if this family mourning the loss of their mother had just received some desperately needed support.

Their brother Lucky approached, saying something she couldn't quite make out. She turned her head away. Eavesdropping was so rude! She attempted to make herself look busy, when, in truth, the ability to look away didn't last long.

Addi peered at Jax one more time, watching as he swept the room with one long glance, and yet did not appear to notice her. She blinked. She was invisible to him—just like old times. That sense of rejection she had experienced as a young adult with stars for dreams returned as if those old feelings had never left. She turned them over in her gut, working hard to tamp them down.

Addi backed away from the table. If only she hadn't volunteered to help Lily. She could have begged off or found a replacement. How she wished she could curl up with a book right now. Or bake something.

Regardless of her commitment to being here today, she had

to get out of this room, to sink back into the reason she had agreed to come in the first place—to work.

Lily had needed help with her mother, Melanie's, memorial and had asked her for her assistance in setting up. They were friends, and that's what friends did. Besides, it was the least she could do for Melanie, who had been kind to her all these years.

So that's what she would do—keep her head down, work, and honor the matriarch of the Cooper family. And that's *all* she would do.

* * *

"Chase is missing."

Not the words Jax expected to hear about his middle brother—one of the twins—minutes after walking into their mother's memorial. Especially when he still had a lot to say to said-AWOL brother. Then again, Jax had learned it was better to live life without too many expectations. Otherwise, the letdown came swiftly, and often without warning.

Chase's twin brother, Lucas aka "Lucky," stared at him, eyes wide, worry all over his face, and Jax felt appropriately chastened. "Sorry," Jax said. "Any idea where Chase went?"

Their sister, Lily, blew back into the room after dashing away to find a box of tissues. She quickly assessed them both with that no-nonsense way of hers and batted a hand at Lucky. "Don't worry about your twin. He's probably watching waves right now."

Lucky's eyes clouded at the brush off. Their sister meant well. Poor woman. Born into a family of five children, four of them male—Jax, Lucky and Chase, and their youngest brother, Nate. Lily had been an old soul since birth, a carbon copy of their mother with her strong body and unwavering opinions.

5

Sometimes it seemed to Jax that Lily fit the oldest child role much better than he did. Not that he didn't at least try to fulfill his big brother duties as often as asked.

Jax cast another gaze on the concerned face of their younger sibling, letting it linger there. Lucas had been known as "Lucky" ever since he had emerged from the womb as a surprise. How the doctor missed that his mother was carrying twins, he would never know. It was understandable Lucky would be worried about his minutes-older twin since they had been inseparable since, well, forever.

"Lily's probably right." Jax ran a hand across a day's growth of whiskers, rare for him, then rested a hand on Lucky's shoulder. "It's a tough day for all of us. Let him be, if that's what he needs."

"Yeah." Lucky swung a look toward the door, as if doing so would cause it to fly open. An eerie silence hung between them. They both knew their mother was never coming back, a thought that tugged at the heart hanging in Jax's chest.

Hopefully, Chase would pull it together soon, though, and return so they could give their mother the send-off she deserved. They all needed to keep it together one last time.

Jax let his hand fall from Lucky's shoulder. He took another look around the place, a large, garage-like room built off their mother's spacious home. A memorial should have solemnity to it, but this one ... he shook his head. Pink, blue, and white balloons. A two-tiered cake. And dogs. Everywhere.

Holding their mother's memorial inside a doggy day care was as upside down as he could fathom. She had opened the place after their father died, and it had brought happiness amid heavy sorrow. It also brought her a reputation for taking in some of the mangiest creatures Jax had ever seen—dogs that had no owners, and therefore, no way to pay. Eventually, she would find them a foster parent or new home, but not before she poured time and effort into them.

On one of their regular video calls once, he'd told her, "You really should keep to just looking after other people's pets, the kind that only visit every once in a while."

She laughed at him, pulled one stray onto her lap, and kissed its ratty little noggin. "Aw, he doesn't mean it, sugar."

Maybe she was right. If it meant seeing his mother smile across the miles, he guessed a mangy mutt or two would be okay. Still, a memorial here? Jax shook his head and followed his sister out of the gathering space and into the kitchen, where a few helpers bustled about.

Lily was saying something about Jax being a sight for sore eyes when he suddenly stopped after spotting ... *her.*

The woman who had broken his heart more than a decade earlier. The sight of her pounded on his heart, pushed tumble-weeds into his head, and made his ever-ready tongue go slack.

Addi Barrett's power over him had not faded, and he hated himself for that.

Jax's gaze lingered on her. The same raven hair pulled into a sleek ponytail. Kind smile as she assisted in the kitchen ... a servant's heart.

He lowered his voice. "What's she doing here, Lily?"

"Who?"

"Addi."

Lily threw a questioning gaze over her shoulder. "What do you mean? She's helping out today. By the way, she's my friend now. Leave her alone."

Jax followed behind his sister, speaking in harsh whispers as she kept moving. "What's that supposed to mean?"

"It means, don't break her heart like you do all the others."

Jax groaned, but Lily kept on going. "I'm serious. Don't flirt.

Don't bother her. She's my friend now. Shoo." She made a sweeping motion with her hand. "Go away."

"Wait. Isn't she married?"

Lily frowned. "I think I'd know if she was."

Addi not married? How did he not know this? Jax leaned against the wall, the news stunning him.

"Come to think of it, I remember that she was briefly engaged." Lily shrugged. "We weren't all that close back then, so I guess I'd forgotten about it."

"You know," Jax said, crossing his arms, "you might have asked me what I thought about Addi helping out today."

Lily turned and her eyes flashed. "Like when I called to ask you your opinion about Mom expanding the doggy care business? About her declining health? Or about any of myriad other questions I texted you only to receive a non-committal 'do whatever makes you happy' response back? Like that, big brother?"

He winced. Admittedly, Jax had been busy the past few years. Building up his clientele in the firm took long hours. Too many nights he would post a sticky note on his computer screen to remind him to call his mother, only to look up from his desk after dark and find it still posted there, taunting him.

Becoming absorbed in his work could be a blessing. But sometimes, when he finally closed the office for the night, a tug of melancholy caught him in the windpipe.

No one was waiting for him at home.

Jax resisted the urge to steal another look at the woman he hadn't seen—or heard from—in years. His sister, whose emotions could turn on a dime, scowled and threw a wet rag into the sink with a little more effort than warranted. He reached out and touched her shoulder. "You know I've always been an ear when you needed one, Lily."

She rolled her eyes. "I had no idea you had problems with Addi. You two used to be the best of friends. I don't know what happened—and frankly, right now I don't care—was probably your fault anyway."

"It's not that I had problems with her." He glanced away. "I, uh, it's been a hard couple of weeks."

"I know."

Jax reached out and pulled his sister into a hug. Lily whimpered into his shirt. She sniffled, then pulled away. "Addi's become the sister I never had. Just leave her be, okay?"

Jax sucked on his bottom lip a moment. "How can I help you?"

Lily stepped away. "Go and grab one of those trays of profiteroles and follow me."

Jax picked up the tray and followed his sister to the main area, forcing thoughts of Addi from his head. Was she still engaged? Or divorced, possibly? He wanted to know, but every time he opened his mouth to ask, he knew—it was none of his business.

He stepped close to his sister. "Tell me again why we're doing this here in a doggy day care? Shouldn't we be in the church?"

"You don't think God is here?"

"Didn't say that."

"Mom would have wanted it this way."

He slowed. "Seriously?"

"She loved it here, Jax." Lily began laying out more food on the expansive table. "Mom spent more time out here with the dogs in her care than she did inside her own house. Not that you'd know. You haven't been around in, what, ten years? Twelve?"

"I visited a handful of times, and Mom flew out to visit me

many times. You know that. And despite my distaste for,"—he gestured to the animals standing guard by their own table of kibble treats—"canines, I always answered Mom's legal questions about the place."

"Whatever." She straightened, jabbed a fist into her side, and glanced about. "The pups need closure. They can say their goodbyes this way."

Jax tilted his head, trying to figure out if a dog could really know that he or she was attending a memorial.

Finally, he said, "And you're sure this has nothing to do with the finances of the place? Can we both admit that Mom's love of animals—and her savings—is what kept this place going?"

Lily directed a glare at him.

He softened the tone of his voice. "Be straight with me—you couldn't afford to close the place today, so that's why you're doing this. Am I correct?"

She narrowed her eyes. "The. Business. Is. Doing. Just. Fine."

Jax stared back at her for a beat, then raised his hands in surrender, while biting back a laugh. "All right. You know what's best."

He had not taken more than two steps before he spotted Addi again. His shoulders stiffened. She had been the number one reason he had left Saltwater Beach, though most didn't know it. Maybe she didn't either. They all thought he'd simply left for college, then stayed away for law school. No one was surprised when he announced he would not be returning home after passing the bar, especially with all his talk of city life.

Only his mother really knew there was more to his decision than that. "You do what you have to do, sugar," she had said back then.

Now he stood rooted, staring at Reason Number One for his lack of travel back home.

"Jax."

He nodded once. "Addi."

She rubbed a tissue between her fingers and avoided long eye contact. "I'm so sorry about your mother."

The lump in his throat began to ache. If he weren't needed here, he would head outside. Get some air. Maybe borrow his sister's truck and take it for a long, long drive.

She continued, sniffling. "She was one of my favorite people, really." A small smile broke out on her face. "Even the meanest dog in town melted around her. One of a kind, she was."

The tsunami of emotion Jax had been holding back rippled forward. He broke eye contact with her and instead swung his gaze around the large space. Distraction was far more comfortable an emotion for him to balance.

Tables brimmed with platters of human food, instead of the usual canine fare of bacon-flavored treats and dog biscuits his mother liked to have around. What he wouldn't do to be attending one of his mother's boring canine meet-and-greets right now by FaceTime.

Addi cleared her throat. "Well, it's good to see you again, Jax, though I wish it were for a different reason."

He glared at her. "Why are you here?"

"Sorry?"

"As I recall, you were engaged to marry." He wanted to say what's-his-name, but resisted. "And were leaving Saltwater Beach."

She pressed her lips together, and a shadow crossed her features. "Yes, well, some plans don't work out."

"So you never left."

11

She looked past him, over his shoulder, and he turned around. Lily was calling her. She turned a sympathetic look on him. "Sorry. I'm here today as a mourner, of course, but also as a favor to your sister. I promised I'd help, so I had better go."

Addi departed, leaving behind the faint scent of her perfume. But all Jax could do was stand there, dumbfounded. She never married? Was here all along, in Saltwater Beach?

Jax pushed away thoughts of Addi. Maybe it was being here again, with familiar faces, that had him swimming in thoughts of yesterday. He glanced behind him where his mother's friends were streaming in through the roll-up door on the north end of the house, past a dozen or so dogs standing in a row, like a receiving line. Addi was right when she said his mother was one of a kind. Those dogs behaved, despite their trainer's absence.

Maybe because of it.

Jax scanned the large room again and caught sight of Lucky and Nate following the others inside. He caught up with them. "Any sign of Chase?"

Lucky hung his head, shaking it side to side, as Nate curled his hand into a fist and punched it into his other hand. "Just like Chase to weasel out of this. When I find him—" he shook his head.

"What?" Jax cracked a smile. "You're gonna grind him into powder? Give him a knuckle sandwich? Make mincemeat out of him?"

"Ha! All of the above, man." Nate, the family's resident cop, shook his head. If anyone had the resources around here to find their brother, it would be him. "I hate this day."

Jax watched as Addi handed one of his mother's coffee mugs to an elderly woman sitting on a folding chair. Even while doing something mundane, and after all this time, she stirred something in him.

"Yeah, I hear you." He pulled his gaze away from the woman who represented his dreams of the past. Objective number one: get in and get out unscathed. "I can't wait for all this to be over myself."

* * *

Jax's expression told Addi all she needed to know: He still thought of her as the old Addi, the tomboy he hung around with in summers and walked to school with the rest of the year. As far as he was concerned, their brush with something more never happened. She had little to no connection to his family and had moved on with her life.

If only.

Truth was, Addi was far from the carefree tomboy she once had been. Not that it mattered. For someone like Jax with family in Saltwater Beach, it surprised her she had not seen him even once in the past decade. Whatever history they had was exactly that: the past.

What she had picked up here and there, though, was that at thirty-one, Jax had built a successful life, the kind he had always talked about when they were kids. At least one of them had. She slowed her movements through the room, digesting that thought. Knowing he had come out of Saltwater unscathed softened her heart along those edges where, if she weren't careful, bitterness would rise.

Addi had loved Jax once. She finally admitted it to herself long ago and then promptly buried it. Perhaps someday, when they were older and fully settled in their own lives, he might learn how much. Despite the sad reason for this gathering, or maybe because of it, she would continue to keep those musings to herself.

Lily rushed by. "Hey, Addi, would you mind refilling the coffee pot?"

"Of course." Addi started for the kitchen, her mind still occupied by thoughts of Jax and how she would handle being this close to him for the next few hours. Her skin still prickled from the jolt of seeing him across the room.

Some things never changed. She and Jax had been glued to each other's sides growing up, starting when she was a sandy tomboy in board shorts and a rash guard, and he a jeans-clad kid on his bike, always doing wheelies in the street. For years, she fantasized he was showing off for her.

But those childhood dreams were long over.

Addi filled the carafe with coffee, being careful not to over-fill it and burn herself. Then she made her way out to the large house addition where mourners had gathered. A bark here, followed by a yap there, drowned out the soft music playing from speakers in every corner. Carefully, she poured coffee into an elderly woman's empty cup.

What was taking so long for the ceremony to begin? Pastor Simon had arrived. All the siblings were here except one. Where was Chase? She had seen him lurking about last night along the quiet stretch of beach where there were no houses. She'd gone there to walk and pray, two activities that had become lifelines for her. She glanced around, careful not to draw attention to herself. As far as she could tell, everyone had shown up but Chase.

She was about to check her phone for the time when, unfortunately, she caught eyes with Jax. He turned away. Addi exhaled. Maybe she was fooling herself. Jax was a lawyer now, handling legal issues that probably took up most of the space in that smart brain of his. Maybe he didn't remember much about her at all.

One thing's for sure: Jax was no longer the wiry teen she remembered, the one with tousled brown hair always in need of a trim. He had aged in the best way, his shoulders broader, his face fuller, not one dark-chocolate lock out of place. And the intensity from his hooded eyes still both frightened her and made her heart turn over in a way that no one else's gaze could.

If she wasn't so preoccupied with the return of the boy next door, she might have noticed someone else approaching. "Well, hello there, beautiful."

She yelped at the sound of the familiar voice and turned, nearly dropping the hot carafe.

Link Grandfield.

Now here was someone who had not changed one bit. Still hulking, cocky, arrogant. He had come home to Saltwater many times since they were kids, but she had usually been able to avoid him after the initial sighting. Until now.

Was he really here to pay his respects to Melanie?

He closed the space between them, his voice a growl, his hot breath suffocating. "How about we blow this stuffy place and go for a drink? My treat."

She'd forgotten one other adjective to describe him: relentless. "Thanks, but no. I'm here to help today."

"Well, then, that's perfect, darlin', 'cause I need some help." He indulged his gaze, allowing it to travel down her face and body then slowly make its way back up again.

She swallowed back a retort. Not that she didn't have one, but for some reason, Addi never found it easy to say exactly what she was thinking.

Link wrapped his meaty hand around her forearm. She tugged it back, but he would not let go. She stared him down, not wanting to make a scene, but this only made him grasp her tighter. Then he laughed, which caused her to yank herself backward, but to no avail.

"Let go of her, Link." Jax showed up next to them, his onyx eyes pointed straight at Link's smug, unwavering grin.

"If it isn't the big guy himself," Link said. He rubbed Addi's arm possessively with his other hand, still holding onto her. Too tightly for her to easily extricate herself. "If we weren't at a funeral, I'd be offended by your assertion, man."

Jax stepped closer. "It's never wise to touch a lady who has not invited you to do so."

Link grinned. "What makes you think she hasn't invited me?"

A web of sweat broke out across Addi's skin. She tugged her arm away from Link's grasp and took a step backward. Jax moved into the space she had vacated, and she noticed something else about him: He'd grown taller, more imposing than ever. She remembered his temper, the way it gave her pause sometimes when they were kids. But this Jax was a force she hadn't seen before.

"I'm fine," she whispered. "Leave it be, Jax."

"You heard the lady." Link nodded at her, but she glanced away. "Addi and I were having a private conversation, so you'll want to move along. Now go. Git." He laughed, displaying yellowed teeth in his wide mouth.

"Leave now." Jax stood with arms crossed, like a sentry between them, unmovable.

Link's smile turned dark, his voice a hiss. "You had your chance years ago, man. It's someone else's turn now."

Jax dropped his arms to his side, one of his hands curled into a fist. He stepped toward Link, and though the guy was a head taller than Jax, he faltered and began falling backward.

Like a beast awakened, Link righted himself and pulled back a fisted hand, but Jax was ready with a block.

Link grunted and swung again, but Jax blocked him a second time, then grabbed his arm and bent it behind him. Jax's low voice snarled. "You are not welcome here now or ever again. I'll see you out."

Link twisted out of Jax's grasp and shook his arm deliberately. "This guy always was a screwup, wasn't he, Addi? Too busy navel gazing to notice what he was missin'." He held up two palms and took a step back. "Well, then, forget it, man. Was going to honor your mother today, say some nice things about the old gal, but you've upset me now. She was a nice lady. Too bad her son didn't inherit her ... disposition."

Jax stepped forward again, but Link shook his head, laughed, then turned and sauntered out.

Addi watched him go, the carafe hanging from her hand like an afterthought.

"You okay?" Jax fixed his gaze on her now, those marble eyes softer somehow.

"Fine. Really." She spoke quietly. "But you haven't changed at all."

"Me?"

She was lying to herself. As much as she wanted to deny it, ever since Jax had walked into this place, she was hopelessly attuned to him. Now, when she looked fully at him, it hurt. They had been friends for so long as kids, she'd hardly had a chance to explore the feelings that grew seemingly for him overnight.

Did he remember how she'd expressed those feelings for him in one rash moment on a humid Friday night that summer?

Addi swallowed, her courage melting away. They weren't

here to rehash the past, but to remember his mother in the most honorable of ways. The last thing she wanted to do was to distract from the solemn meaning of the day, but oh, he was melting her resolve.

Without warning, Lily launched herself between Addi and Jax. "So, I think we need to get started." She turned her chin and shot a look at Jax. "We'll just have to show Chase the video later." A couple of dogs punctuated Lily's announcement with high-pitched barks.

Jax acknowledged his sister briefly, then turned those smoky eyes on Addi again. She blinked, willing them away from her consciousness. Lily was right. Jax was a heartbreak, and she'd best be avoiding him at all costs.

She carried the half-empty carafe toward the kitchen, intending to buy some time while refilling it. For good reason, Addi had let go of her feelings for Jax years ago. And she wasn't about to allow herself to be dragged back into a world that would only bring her heartache when Jax walked away from her ... again.

Chapter Two

The nostalgia of heat and sand and salty air hit Jax's senses as he belted himself into Lily's meticulously cared for truck. Their father had once owned it, but nearly every part of that memory of him had been scrubbed clean. No more surfboards in the back or sand embedded in floorboards. Jax didn't feel the need to sanitize sweat from the seats, as he once had. He strained to remember what it was like to sit next to Dad on a Saturday morning as he watched the waves.

The memory appeared like a warm light.

Through the windshield, Jax took one more look toward the beach, scanning for any sign of his brother Chase. A prick of worry about Chase's whereabouts had wakened him in the middle of the night. If Chase wanted to stay away for his own reasons, he would respect that, but coming home put his roots into perspective. He wanted to do his due diligence and double check the area.

Last night, he and his other siblings had lingered after their mother's memorial, all of them wondering when their brother would traipse into the place with a bevy of excuses. Regardless of his non-appearance, the ritual had brought with it some healing as they consumed the final scraps of cookies and muffins, emptied the last of bottles of wine, and shared memories that, although had been expected to bring tears, brought on uproarious laughter instead. Mostly, anyway.

He still couldn't forget the picture Lily painted of their mother, allowing one dog to pull her as she rode a bike. Apparently, she had held on for dear life as the frisky golden retriever went into a gallop down the beach path as onlookers scattered. But that was their mom—willing to try about anything.

Jax's smile faded as he pulled in front of Barrett Hardware in downtown Saltwater. Some shops along Main Street hadn't changed, such as the shoe repair place and corner bookshop with its neon sign in the window screaming BOOKS!

But the candy shop was long gone, and in its place a coffee shop with a garish name—hadn't Lily mentioned she frequented it? And the dentist's office, with the animated tooth in the window, now housed a furniture design store.

Then there was the old hardware store that had been rebuilt after a nasty fire. His father had owned the building once. Strangely, the shop didn't look all that different on the outside now from when he was a kid running into the place to pick up surf wax or a toilet plunger for his dad.

The owner had resurrected the shop to look like it always had. The bold BH logo on its awning was only slightly less daunting than it was to him back then—but that was mainly because of who the owner was.

Jax exhaled, remembering. So much bad blood between his father and the store's owner. All that had disappeared now, of course, with his father's death more than eight years ago.

Jax groaned, not caring to revisit any of the old griefs.

Truth was, he hadn't paid all that much attention to the two sparring men. His parents, being the forgiving sort, had shielded him and his siblings from most of it. Besides, he was heading out of town around then to attend college, and frankly, the months before were nothing but a blur to him.

No matter now anyway. He was here to pick up patching compound to fix some holes in the walls inside the family home—especially in areas where canines had made their mark. "Might as well get it over with," he muttered.

"I know you're here to handle the legal stuff," Lily had said last night, after putting away the last dish, "but this place could use some light remodeling."

"And you want *me* to handle that?"

She had laughed then and kissed him on the cheek, apparently finished with being annoyed with him. "Tag. You're it."

Unlike his father, who could do an early morning surf check, take a two-hour surf *board* meeting, then go to his workshop to build shelving or cabinets all afternoon or give subs work, Jax had not inherited the construction gene. Neither had any of his brothers really. Lucky and Chase were as different as twins could be. Lucky created apps and worked in the dog daycare, and Chase took work as a tugboat captain whenever he could find it (when he wasn't hiding from his family, that is). Nate fought criminals on the local police force, and Lily? Hm ... what did Lily do for work these days?

Jax made a mental note to ask her, while stuffing down the unease of not knowing what his only sister did to pay the bills.

He released a sigh. Regardless of his inability to remember some of life's details, he was determined to help with whatever Lily asked of him today—even if that meant scraping walls and filling holes. So after checking in with his office staff this morning, Jax headed toward the hardware store, ready to tackle those minor repairs around his mother's home.

Now, as he sat in the truck, looking through the windshield at the store, he swallowed back the growing reticence he had been feeling about this little errand. Addi's father owned this shop. Or, he did when they were kids—and after the fire—so he assumed nothing had changed. Like the fact that Addi's dad could be meaner than a dog who'd missed out on feeding time.

Jax whistled. Maybe the man had parted with the place after all. Four years of college, three years of law school, and another three years of clawing his way up the rungs toward partnership in a big firm, and yet, still, Jax was afraid of the grumpy dad of a girl he once ... well, he once cared for.

He exited the car and stepped inside. The old bell on the door coupled with the strong smell of freshly cut wood mixed with oil and metal and wax caused him to feel all of sixteen again. Man. For a shop that had been rebuilt less than a dozen years ago, it hadn't changed. Unlike himself.

Instinctively, Jax wandered down an aisle, found a small tub of Spackle, a pack of putty knives, and then made his way to the paint counter where he planned to order a color mix to blend in with the walls in strategic places.

Heavy footsteps approached. Jax raised his chin to find Vic Barrett standing in silence, chunky black glasses on the edge of his nose, assessing Jax. The man hadn't changed much, except for a wider girth, perhaps, and more salt on his thinning hair. But one thing that he didn't recognize was the man's size. He was smaller somehow, yet still unnerving.

"Good morning, sir."

"Hm. You're the lawyer." His tone conveyed that this was neither a question nor an affirmation.

"Yes. I am."

"How is the legal business these days?" From anyone else, the question might have sounded friendly. Neighborly, even. But the way the older man said the words, peppered with sarcasm, Jax could tell he had a problem with the law. He would have to ask Nate for confirmation of this.

Instead, Jax simply said, "Thank you for asking, sir. Yes, my firm is doing well."

Vic said nothing. A man of sparse words he could handle, but the familiar frown and steady stare a little less so. He managed it fine in a deposition or from across a courtroom where he regularly faced opposition. But Jax never was too fond of the way Mr. Barrett regularly showed just how little he cared for him.

If at all.

Jax tipped his head toward the man of few words. "A pleasure seeing you again, sir."

"Is it?"

Jax forced a smile, growing weary at this game. "I came in to order some touch-up paint." He held up the small, nearly empty can that he had brought with him, hoping the man could either find the formula for it or match it himself.

Mr. Barrett took the can from him, frowning like a contractor who had just been asked to move a shelf up three inches. He almost expected the man to sneer and say, "It'll cost ya."

But Addi's father only turned away from him and disappeared around the corner. Jax released a breath and fought the urge to sprint right back out the door. Whoever said you can't go back again had never shaken in his flip-flops in front of ol' Mr. Barrett at the local hardware store on a Saturday morning.

Instead of following his gut instinct, though, i.e., running right out the door, Jax wandered down an aisle with all kinds of kitsch for home decor. None of the stuff seemed to fit here, but maybe Addi's mother had inspired the items in this aisle. Wood-painted signs, rose and lavender candles, wire statues of children riding bicycles—all of it would look out of place in his condo back home with its shiny quartz countertops and black cabinetry.

Down another aisle, he slowed to look at baskets full of stuffed toys for dogs and cats until he ran across several fat pink teething rings—the same ones he had noticed in his mother's home. How often had she stopped in here to peruse this aisle and spend her sparse resources on "something fun for the kids," aka her favorite local mutts?

Jax had been wandering awhile, lost in his memories, when a gust from a nearby open window brought him to the present. What was taking the old man so long?

He peered around the corner. Next to the ancient cash register was the can he had brought with him today, along with a new gallon of paint. He glanced around and neither heard nor saw old man Barrett. The man hadn't even said that he was done mixing Jax's paint.

Jax frowned, pulled two bills from his wallet, and laid them on the counter. Then he glanced around the empty store once more before stepping outside, still shaking his head.

Minutes later, he stepped into his mother's home just as Addi entered, her sing-song voice slicing through the thick air around them. "Here we are ..."

Their gazes clashed, her words trailing away.

Jax shot a questioning look at Lily, but he spoke to Addi. "Did my sister recruit you to clean up? Thought we already made good work of it last night."

Lily scoffed. "She's not the housekeeper, Jax. Addi works for the daycare."

"The day ..."

"Doggy daycare," Addi reminded. "I was just helping out your sister in the kitchen last night since we're friends."

"Buddies," Lily piped up.

"Pals," Addi said.

Jax tilted his head to the side. "So you two really are friends now?"

Both women laughed as if he were the butt of some private joke.

Lily took the leashes from Addi's hands and coiled one of them around her hand. "Plus, she's an amazing baker—she made those cookies we all consumed last night. I keep telling her she should open a bakery in town. We sorely need one around here."

Addi smiled kindly. "Thanks, but you could get about anything you want at the grocery store."

Lily laughed. "Not baked with love, like you make it."

Addi cracked up. She noticed the can in Jax's hand.

"Your father mixed it for me."

She nodded. "And how did that go?"

Jax shrugged. "He's a man of few words."

"I meant the paint. Is it what you wanted?"

"Oh. Right." He held the can up, comparing the sample smudge to the wall. "Looks good to me."

"I'd say it's pretty perfect." She paused. "About Daddy ... he's had it rough the past two years, what with Momma passing away."

Jax's face jolted a look at her. He hadn't heard this news, and a sense of loss again tugged at him. He couldn't expect to come back to Saltwater to find that little had changed.

As he thought about it, though, it wasn't a complete surprise that Addi's mom had passed. From what he recalled, she had often been sickly—isn't that the way his mother always phrased it? Admittedly, he never knew what ailed her.

"I'm sorry to hear that, Addi." How much more had he missed in the past decade that he hadn't realized?

"Thank you."

Lily nodded at the can of paint. "Addi's been around her dad's hardware store, so I'm sure she could offer some tips, but she's on duty." His sister gave him a pointed look. "So leave her alone."

Jax laughed. "How hard could it be to spread some Spackle and paint over a divot made by a dog's claws?"

Addi's chin lifted. "Depends on how deep the dog dug those claws into the wall."

"Your father didn't suggest I buy anything else."

"Well, maybe you didn't tell him what you were planning to do."

Jax shrugged. "It'll be easy enough. I'm sure."

Addi narrowed her eyes at him.

Lily interceded. "Good. Great. Fabulous." She swept her hand at him. "Get going already."

An awkward quiet fell in the room after that and he wanted to kick himself. His legal assistant, Tory, told him he sometimes carried over his short and curt ways to his personal life. He scolded her for eavesdropping—a regular occurrence—but he suspected that if she were here right now, she would be mouthing to him: *See? That's what I mean.*

"Well," Addi said, turning her attention on Lily. "I better get back inside too. The Garcias just dropped off Gracie and you know how her anxiety is. Poor thing."

When she'd gone, Jax stood rooted in place. He snagged his sister's gaze. "Question."

"How do you do that?"

"Do what?"

"Change the subject quickly. First you shut down the room with that know-it-all-attitude and stern look of yours, then you switch to whatever is on your mind."

He narrowed his eyes. "Why didn't you tell me that Addi was here?"

"I told you yesterday, she works—"

"I mean before I arrived. You could have prepared me for seeing her again after all these years."

"Why would I do that?

Jax leaned a jeans-clad hip against the wall. He raised his eyes. "And why didn't she get married?"

Lily crossed her arms. "What does it matter to you? I understand you two were buddies growing up, maybe even had cute little crushes on each other at some point, but shoot, that was *years* ago. You're a highfalutin big city lawyer—"

"Oh, come on."

"What?"

"No one, and I mean *no one*, uses the term *highfalutin* anymore."

Lily's face went deadpan. "I just did."

"This whole conversation is odd."

Lily peeled a look up at him. "Is that what you say whenever you don't like someone's response? 'Your honor, the plaintiff is odd. His lawyer is odd. And for that matter, this whole case is ... odd!'"

"What's gotten to you anyway? All I asked is why didn't she get married? When I left Saltwater, that was the plan. For all I knew, she was living somewhere behind a white picket fence and running after a house full of kids."

"Then why do you care? Besides, you were engaged too, if

you recall." Her tone turned gentler. "Maybe the question should be, why didn't you get married, big brother?"

A rush of painful memories sucked the wind right out of him. He would prefer not to think about his breakup with Mara ever again. What good would it serve to revisit such an uncomfortable memory anyway? Being left at the altar—well, the day before he would've been waiting at that altar—wasn't something a person should revisit.

Some, like his sister, probably thought he had it coming. That he got what he deserved when Mara broke up with him. But they mistook being selective as a sign he was afraid to commit.

Jax hauled in a breath. He turned questions on others for a living and wasn't about to allow his sister to do that to him. He leaned his hip against the counter and crossed his arms in front of his chest. "My guess is you know exactly what happened to end Addi's engagement."

His sister did that little hand wave into the air when she considered a matter closed.

"Lily?"

She tilted her head, like a teacher about to scold a wayward student. "You two were children the last time you saw each other. You've made your life, and she's made hers. Let it go."

"Listen, if I wanted relationship advice, I would ask you for it."

"Oh, really, Jax? Because you're not exactly the king of sharing your life with anyone, especially your family."

"Why are we fighting again?"

"Because you're being a dumb big brother right now." The door swung open and a mid-size brown-haired dog skidded in and sniffed Jax's sneakers before curling up on one of his feet. "Guess at least one somebody likes you though."

He shot a look at her. Really? She was just going to tell him he was dumb and move on?

The dog continued its mini-investigation around Jax's feet. Everyone knew that, for whatever reason, he had never really taken to dogs. Wasn't afraid of them, just didn't connect with canines like so many others did. Especially his parents.

"Hey." He attempted to lift his foot, the animal now dead weight on top of it. "Go on now."

"Aw, Jax. Have a heart. Olive just wants to say hello." Lily laughed.

The dog yawned and lifted her head to look at him. Jax sucked in a breath. "She only has one eye."

Lily pressed her lips together and nodded.

"What happened to her?"

"Likely an accident. She gets along fine though."

"Well, this is unfortunate." He looked at Lily. "How long will she be here today?"

"Meaning?"

"When will her owner be picking her up?" Lily continued to stare at him with a quizzical look. He added, "Sorry. Should I have said parent?"

"Sadly, Olive's human mom has passed away."

"I don't understand."

"I had no idea that you didn't know. Olive was Mother's foster dog. Well, unofficially."

"Mom's? No." He shook his head. "Mom didn't have a dog. Well, other than the ones she babysat."

"In other words, she never mentioned her to you." Lily rolled her eyes. "Olive was abandoned at the shelter, and when they couldn't find a home for her, Mom took her in. The plan was—or is—to find her a permanent home eventually."

"So ... she lives here."

"Generally, that's how it works. And, for now, yes."

Jax let out a long *shew*. Olive leaned her head against his shin, but he refused to look down. "How did I not know that? Besides, family dogs are male."

Lily clucked her tongue. "That old saying again. The guys in this family always wanted boy dogs."

"Correction. I wanted no dogs."

"That's right. You never were fond of animals, were you?"

"It's not that I wasn't fond of them. Just didn't like having them around very much."

"Same difference." Lily quirked a smile. "I have to say, though, she likes you. Weird taste, that one. By the way, she might need surgery. Hence the need for a permanent home with someone who can handle that."

Jax dropped a fist to the table, which only made Lily laugh. "No wonder this place is bleeding money. But I suppose that explains why Mom never mentioned her to me."

Lily smiled. "Maybe. But I also think Mom enjoyed having her little secrets, especially from all of us. Though she never really could keep much from me."

Jax crossed his arms. "She can't stay here, just like you can't keep running this place anymore now that Mom is, well—"

"Gone?"

Jax and Olive sighed in tandem. Lily gave him a smile. He was about to relent and squat down to pet the mutt when Addi came careening back in through the door.

"So sorry! I hadn't realized Olive was strong enough to push open that swinging door." Addi scooped up the dog, who let out a small whine. She pressed her mouth against the dog's hairy face. "When did you learn to do that, my love?"

Lily interjected. "She's been all moony eyed with Jax in here."

Addi quirked a tiny smile, but kept her attention on Olive. "Giving that eye a workout, then. Good girl!"

Jax dropped his hands at his sides. The home repairs could wait for now. He should have probably just hired someone anyway, though his sister would have piled on the guilt if he had.

He darted a look toward a window, its blinds pulled up. Maybe fresh air and a quick call to the office would clear his head. One thing he knew: standing this close to Addi would do anything but that.

* * *

"Oh, good! You called." Tory from his office had a flare for the dramatic, though he had to admit, sometimes it was warranted. He hoped this wasn't one of those times.

"Any messages for me?"

"Is the sky blue? What a question! This place has been nonstop with phone calls. And mail! You're getting so much mail you'd think the US Postal Service offered a sale on stamps. Man, I've already had two paper cuts opening it all up."

Others in his firm didn't take too well to Tory's incessant play-by-plays, but she was an excellent assistant. Detailed. Good writer. He'd heard enough horror stories from other attorneys he knew he ought to count his blessings rather than nitpick.

He had walked away from the house, far enough to not be heard. Now he took a seat on a rock overlooking the sea, as this was obviously going to take a while. "Go ahead, then."

"Well, first"—she lowered her voice—"were you aware Todd and Gema were seeing each other? It's the story everybody's not talking about right now, but they all know."

He flicked a glance at gnats circling the air above scrubby beach grass. "Does this have anything to do with the pile of mail and phone messages I have on my desk?"

"No, it doesn't, but you've been gone for days." She drew out the word. "So I knew you'd want to be filled in."

"Just get to the messages."

"Right. You got it. First, Mary's been working on discovery for the Platt case and just heard back from ..."

Jax listened as Tory went through message after message. Her voice had changed, and he knew she was irked at him for not leaning into the gossip she so lavishly dished up. But he didn't have time for it. Not with his mother's estate details and his brother's curious absence keeping him here in Saltwater.

"...and, oh, Mr. Patterson wants to know when you'll be returning to Chicago."

His ears perked at the mention of his boss's name. How many messages had he missed before realizing he had been daydreaming? "Slow down. What's that about Brock?"

"Mr. Patterson has stopped by twice while you've been gone. Of course, I've reminded him that your mother died— God rest her soul—and that you would be away for quite some time."

"I'll be home as soon as I'm able. Please remind him of that."

"Well, yes, of course. That's what I meant. I have your back, Jax. I told him you've been checking in regularly— although let's be honest here, I've hardly heard from you."

Jax rolled his eyes upward. He could do without all the asides. Really.

"So anyway, he didn't leave you a message to call him or anything, but what—"

"Next time he stops in, tell him I plan to be back in

Chicago within two weeks. Max. In the meantime, please let him know I am available by phone and will be working from here whenever possible."

"Nobody expects that!"

"If there's nothing more, I'll sign off now." After a reluctant sigh from Tory, Jax hung up, questions about Brock Patterson rummaging through his head. He opened his phone and began scrolling through his email, looking for any sign the head of the firm had made a decision about Jax's future.

He had been sitting there so long, lost in thought with the beating sun on his back that he hadn't heard steps approaching until they were nearly upon him. He looked up with a jolt.

Addi. She appeared to be as startled by his presence as he was by hers. "Hey." He dropped his phone onto his thigh.

She mustered a small smile, her eyes darting about. If he wasn't mistaken, she looked ready to run off, like a wounded deer.

"Out for a walk?" *Smooth, Jax, smooth.* He cleared his throat and stood.

"I, well, yes. I'm taking a break, and thought I'd, well, look for Chase."

"My brother?"

She frowned, her forehead bunching. "He's still missing, so ..."

"You could say that, but I tend to think he is staying away on purpose."

"Why would you think that?"

Jax sighed. "It's a hunch. He's always been a kind of brooding guy. Not sure if you remember that from when we were kids."

She was quiet a moment. Then finally, "Well, maybe so.

But I have some time now, so I thought I'd walk out to the old lifeguard stations, the ones that aren't used anymore."

He whistled. "Those old towers are still out there?"

"They are."

"And you think he's hiding out on those relics?"

She let out an exasperated gasp. Not the first time his questioning had elicited such a response. "It's worth a try, Jax."

He considered her. Spotting Addi at his mother's memorial had stung. She had rejected him a dozen years ago, and as far as he knew, had moved on with her life. As had he.

As it turned out, she had been here all along and now wanted to spend her free time looking for his missing brother. Interesting. He cleared his throat. "I suppose it is. I am appropriately chastised."

A small smile played on her lips.

"May I join you?"

She shrugged and eventually nodded. After an awkward start, they walked quietly, side by side. He knew this path still, the curves unchanged. The earthy smells of scrub pine and wild lupine met his senses over and over again, and at times, it almost felt like he had never left Saltwater. Or maybe Saltwater had never left him.

"My father used to let us run around out here when we were little. Lots of places to hide, especially for ambushing siblings."

That got a smile out of her.

"I know."

He turned, taking in the way the sun's rays highlighted flecks of color in her dark hair.

"Maybe you don't remember. He let me tag along."

He was quiet for a moment. "I guess I was thinking about the Addi I knew long after that ... when we were in high school." She wore a poker face, but he sensed he had hurt her feelings. "I'm sorry I didn't remember that you spent a lot of time with us when we were little."

She shrugged. "It's fine. You're right—I stopped hanging out with most of you by the time we were teenagers and never came out here then." Addi shaded her eyes and looked toward the horizon. "Your dad sure did like to surf."

He followed her gaze. "That he did. I never really followed him in that regard though."

"I remember."

"Tagged along occasionally. He loved to drive far down the coast to some old oil piers and surf there. He'd camp along the way, and sometimes the twins and I would go along. Nate was too young." He slowed. "Remember the stray dogs my dad would pick up sometimes?"

She tilted her chin, as if thinking back. "I think I do."

"Hadn't thought of that in a long time. Dad would pick up a stray dog here and there. Feed it some jerky and let it play on the beach. If he couldn't find its owner, he'd take it to the rescue up on the hill." Jax contemplated this, the memory coming through like a well-worn film. "I never really took to any of the animals. Not the way Dad did."

Addi slowed as they exited through a small stand of trees on the edge of the hardened path. She shaded her eyes with a hand, searching the old towers for sign of his brother. A twinge of envy prodded him—had she kept an eye out for him when he'd gone off to college the way she searched for Chase? He mentally pushed his musing away.

"I never thought to look here," he said.

"Where have you looked so far?"

He mulled that. "I briefly scanned the beach yesterday, but

35

otherwise I haven't thought much about where he might have gone."

She turned to face him, her green eyes searching his face. With that one look, she managed to burrow under his skin. "Why is that, Jax?"

"My brother ..." He pulled his gaze away from hers. "Chase has always been a tough one to figure out." How could he explain the dynamics of a jumble of boys growing up in one house to a woman who had never been forced to live in such an environment?

"You're all tough to figure out, if you ask me."

He snapped his gaze to her, but she had already begun walking again. The lifeguard towers had been here since they were kids. Any other town council would have had them torn down and either destroyed or dismantled for parts, but not Saltwater. Life moved slowly here, unlike so many other beach towns that had been overtaken by highways and high rises of steel and glass. This one still meandered in places.

That's one of the reasons he left—to live where life moved at a pace faster than a sand crab burrowing its way out of deep sand. As if to illustrate that point. Jax's phone dinged. "I should—"

"Get that. I know." Addi didn't look back but continued to trudge toward the grouping of towers.

Jax halted in place, one hand on his phone, watching flyaways of her dark hair catch on the breeze. His phone dinged again and he huffed a sigh, wishing the progress of nearby cell-phone towers hadn't found Saltwater. Tory had texted him.

Mr. Patterson asked me if I talked to you about the Rosa case. I messed up and forgot to tell you what's going on with it. Ack. And now he wants to talk to you. Maybe you should call him? (Sorry.)

So much for having his back. He grimaced. Chivalry told him to go after Addi and make sure she was safe among that ancient pile of wood out there. But the part of him that could read her body language, with its stiff movements and crossed arms, held him in check. Addi didn't want him around.

Just like that summer before he left Saltwater for good.

Well. She may not want him around, but he wasn't about to leave her out here all alone while she searched for *his* brother. Jax stayed put, but pulled out his phone, found his office phone number, and placed a call.

Chapter Three

Addi had done her haughty best yesterday to get Jax to turn around and head back home, but it hadn't worked. Even with a phone sticking out of his ear, he had stayed with her as she looked through the lifeguard towers for any sign of his missing brother.

Chase. A niggling of something told her things weren't quite right with the Cooper family's middle child. She had no reason to say that—just a hunch. A lot of good hunches were, though, when no one else seemed to be troubled by them.

She hadn't seen Chase since the night before the memorial. He had been so downcast, but nothing out of the ordinary given the situation. She'd always had a soft spot for the Coopers' middle kid, well, one of the twins anyway. Some might have thought Lucky was the one to worry over, but she knew better. Chase had skeletons she knew about, though she doubted that had anything to do with missing his mother's memorial.

As someone who had lost her mother, too, she suspected Chase was just very sad and needed time to process.

Addi sat outside on the back porch of the Cooper home

and business, brushing Olive's wavy, cocoa-brown fur. Thankfully, Lucky and two teen assistants were inside with the critters who had been dropped off today. The youngest twin was a sweetheart and genuinely kind to the dogs and their parents.

Nothing was the same, and yet when the beach wind whispered over her, the old days came back on the breeze. At this moment, she was having an easier time remembering the long ago past than she could more recent times. She remembered running out there through that brush, her hair kicking up behind her, without a care in the world.

One recent thing she wouldn't soon forget was the look on Jax's face yesterday when she retrieved Olive from the kitchen. If it weren't so sad, she would have laughed. How could he not love dogs when the world was clearly a better place with them in it?

Addi strained to remember how Jax had acted around animals when they were kids, but nothing came to mind. Probably because her memories of an older teen overtook the ones of her younger self. Older Addi was too crazy about Jax to notice his lack of interest in creatures.

Well, her bad.

What she did recall acutely, almost as if they were still teenagers, was the way he hovered over his younger brothers, always calling them in for supper or throwing the ball around with the twins or helping Nate with his homework. He'd had something she did not—siblings—and seemed to take the role of big brother seriously.

The Cooper boys and Lily had been like family to her. A distant one, but family just the same. Their laughter and late-night skylarking made the difficulties in her own home easier to face somehow.

She sighed. Life with the Coopers for neighbors had

become synonymous with summer fun extending into fall, twilight distractions that made the school year bearable, and at one point, a slow unravel of friendship into ... something more.

At least, she had thought so.

She wasn't all that surprised Jax had not returned to Saltwater Beach after college to make a life here. Not that she hadn't entertained the thought, then quickly brushed it away. Would his return after her engagement ended have altered anything between them? She bit the fleshy part of her inner lip. Probably not.

The door to the back porch opened. Jax stepped outside, his hands ladened with supplies. He walked toward a small table, a ripple of memory igniting her. She always loved the way he moved. Shoulders upright, confident, a bit of swagger, but not so much that it was a turn off.

He spotted her watching him and slowed. His phone was glaringly absent. "Hey."

"Hey yourself."

Olive's ears perked, though she remained prone in a sliver of sunlight. She opened her eye and lay there, staring, as if seeing a mirage.

Jax dumped the tools—brushes, paint can, putty—onto the table. "I'll be starting out here." He gestured toward a gash in the house's wooden siding.

Addi stood. "Sounds good to me. I'll take Olive inside so she doesn't bother you."

As if to show her independence, Olive hopped up and trotted over to see what Jax was doing. She sniffed the leg of his jeans. Jax didn't shake her off this time, but neither did he offer to pet her.

"C'mon, girl." Addi sighed. "C'mon, Olive!"

"Addi?"

"Yes?"

"Maybe I'll see you inside later."

"Okay. Sure." Olive followed Addi inside, but not before lending a reluctant look toward Jax.

An hour later, Lucky brought a couple of dogs—a cockapoo named Teal and a boxer named Squirt—into the pen where Addi had been throwing a ball to a small pack that had grown tired of each other.

"My brother's making a mess all over the place, so I'm consolidating. You can go now, if you want. I'll stay in here."

"Thanks. I think I'll go for a walk, then check in with Lily to see what she has for me." Olive squeezed out of the gate next to her and she sighed. She turned back. "Lucky? I'll take our Olive with me."

As they snaked through the house, it didn't take long for the resident one-eyed pup to find Jax, who had moved inside. He was kneeling in front of an interior wall now and using a rag to wipe off excess putty. "She's quite interested in what you're doing over there."

"Oh yeah?" Jax kept working as Olive sniffed around. She neither jumped all over him nor growled. Instead, she sat dutifully next to him and appeared to be watching intently as he worked.

"Pretty unusual."

He turned a look over his shoulder. "That she would be interested in me?"

Addi's cheeks heated from the fire in that simple question. "That she would sit so quietly and watch. She's a sweetheart, but she also has a dark side."

"This precious baby?" He glanced down at her. "I can't imagine."

"Well, imagine it. Oh, and a little hint from me to you—

keep the lid on that paint can closed or she'll make herself at home with its contents."

Jax smiled.

"Okay, c'mon, girl. Let's let Jax get back to work—"

"She's fine. Let her stay." Jax sat back on his haunches and touched Olive's head. If emojis were real, a flutter of red hearts might have emerged into the air right above that hairy little head of hers.

"You old softy."

Jax glanced up at her, and his brows dipped.

"Does that not play well with your hard-nosed lawyer image?"

He threw a look upward, laughing.

Addi shrugged. "What can I say? I've never seen this side of you. You know, the dog-loving side."

Jax's eyes held hers. "A guy can change."

After a long second, she found her voice again. "I suppose he could."

Jax continued to smooth Olive's fur with his hand. "I had no idea you'd be here," he finally said. "Neither my sister nor mother mentioned you were working at the daycare."

"Honestly, they didn't mention you much either."

He winced. "Ouch."

"I didn't mean it in a biting way." Addi bent to give Olive a few more pets. Spoiled animal. "Your mother was so focused on all the dogs, and your sister is ..."

"Frenetic? Obsessive? A whirling dervish?"

Addi cracked a smile. "She's got a lot on her plate."

"You're kind."

"Lily and I have become good friends. It's funny, but we weren't all that close in school. People change, I guess, and we have a lot of the same interests." Addi caught eyes with Jax. She realized how close they were standing, and slowly backed away while clearing her throat. "Anyway, she has a big heart."

Jax gave her a slow nod. "True. Something I probably don't give her enough credit for."

"Well, you are a dude, after all."

He coughed a laugh. "What does that have to do with anything?"

She shrugged, her smile intact.

In mock anger, he threw down the rag he had been working over the wall. There. There was the kid she once knew, the one who would holler her full name—Addison Marie Barrett—into a crowded school hallway, as if she was one scolding away from detention.

She used to get so mad at that!

But secretly, she liked the attention. Addi didn't have much of that at home with her father working long days and nights and her mother so sick all the time.

Not to mention the fire that eventually brought them all to the breaking point.

Mercifully, her cellphone trilled. Her father's name appeared on the screen. Addi turned her head away from Jax to take the call. "Uh-huh, yes. I'm talking to Jax now—"

She looked over her shoulder to find Jax's gaze on her. He turned back to his work, with Olive settled in next to him.

Addi dragged her attention back to the phone. "But I still have more to do—" She kept the tone of her voice in check. Addi had learned over time that her father stayed calmer whenever she kept her voice steady. "Sure. I'll be there as soon as possible."

"Everything okay?" Jax asked like someone who suspected there might be a problem.

She stood and dusted herself off. "Sure is. If you're really okay with me leaving Olive here, I'm going to duck inside to let Lily know I've got to help my father with something."

Jax gasped, but it was so fake she could barely contain a laugh. "You're going to leave me alone with her?"

For her part, Olive lifted her head briefly, eyed Jax, then settled back into the shape of an S with a fluttery little sigh.

Addi grabbed her purse and flung it over her shoulder. "Somehow I think the two of you will manage."

Minutes later, Addi pulled up in front of her father's hardware store. Thankfully, she'd driven over to the Coopers' place with the thought she might need her car later. That inkling was getting louder lately, and she wasn't sure what to do about it.

As she approached, Pastor Simon stepped out of the store, certain relief on his face. "Good to see you, Addi."

She nodded, her smile tentative. "Pastor."

He lowered his voice. "I'm glad you're here."

"Is he ... is everything okay?"

Pastor Simon's penetrating gaze, the one he whipped out during sermons to a rapt congregation, met hers. "I think it will be, but I'd like to talk privately with you soon. Please call the office and let Annette know when you're available. Will you do that?"

"Of course."

He nodded and walked away, but not before first flashing a sympathetic smile in her direction.

Emotion boiled up from within as she shoved open the door. Inside, the store smelled like a skunk had wandered through it after gleefully spraying the neighborhood. Oh, joy.

"There's my ray of sunshine!"

"You're smoking again." And probably a lot more than just smoking ...

"Can't get anything past you, now can I?" Her father

drummed his hands on the counter, clapped them together, then shot fingers like guns at his daughter.

She hated that weird, sarcastic expression he wore on his face after a bender. Most people passed out for a long nap, but not her father, no. First, he'd play drums on any surface for whoever would listen. Then he would chatter on as if he'd consumed several espressos, one right after the other.

And then he would fall asleep in his office, whether the store was closed—or still open.

For a half second, Addi froze, wondering what it might have been like to have a father who could naturally have a good time. Someone who could laugh easily or shut the store down early and say, "Let's go get some ice cream and walk on the beach tonight, Addison!"

She had seen that sort of thing from Jax's dad, Mike, but never from her own father. Well, not unless he had smoked a ton of pot first or pounded back the beers.

As soon as the thoughts flooded her mind, shame followed. *Honor thy father and mother.* The verse from Scripture had been a guiding one for her, but lately she found it very, very difficult to follow.

She breathed in deeply, stepped behind the counter, and removed her coat.

"You stayin' awhile?" His words were beginning to slur.

Addi put her arm around her father's shoulder and gently led him away from the counter and into the back where he kept a cot for himself. It had been there ever since she was little, and she had never once thought it strange.

But as she ushered him over to the rickety old thing that he would likely nap on for the next few hours, she began to question everything she had accepted as normal.

* * *

"I'm sick." Lily sneezed.

Jax slid a tissue box down the dining room table toward her. Two days had passed since he began his quest to fill all the holes and touch up the paint around the house. He hadn't noticed how sparse his sister's presence had become.

Maybe that's because he had been fielding calls from his office the entire time, while trying to ignore Addi's presence with very little success. More than once he had found himself sitting back on his haunches, staring into space like some kind of lovesick teenager.

Lily sneezed again, and Jax jolted. He frowned. "Maybe you shouldn't have been traipsing around in the cold last night looking for Chase." He crossed his arms now, not mentioning he and Addi had also attempted to smoke him out. "He's a big boy, Lily. He'll come home when he's ready."

Even as he said it, a small part of him wondered if there was something bigger going on with his brother. Addi had said as much to him the other day when they had been lurking about those old lifeguard towers. He should have been pondering that, rather than allowing him to linger on thoughts of a girl he wouldn't see again once the house issues were taken care of and he was back in his office, with its view of the Chicago River.

"A lot you know." She sniffled and stepped across the dining room in a robe much too thick for summer. She removed candlesticks from the table and tucked them into a hutch. "Mom would have never allowed him to be gone this long without checking in."

He stood and followed her into the kitchen. "What would she have done about it?"

"One thing's for sure," Lily said over her shoulder, "she

wouldn't be ignoring the fact that one of her twin sons had not shown up or called for days. Our mama would have done far more than I have. She would've been knocking on every door and even posting Most Wanted posters at the post office."

He cracked a grin at this. Their mother was a force, no doubt about that. She'd even talked the local planning department into giving her a permit for her doggy daycare—against his advice. "If they give them out like candy for human daycares," she'd said, "I should be able to get one for my small doggy operation."

And she did.

"If it helps," Jax said to Lily, "I called the port office to see if he had taken any last-minute gigs on the water."

"And?"

"Nothing."

She swung around, a fist jabbing her waist. "So we just stop looking?"

Jax released a weary breath. Lily was right. Their mother didn't give up easily. Perhaps this is where Lily got her stamina for long hours and squirrelly animals. Surely this isn't what she wanted to be doing with her time.

She frowned and released another sigh as she turned and dragged a large bag of dog food from the pantry.

"Here," he said. "Let me help." She relinquished her hold. Jax lugged the massive bag onto the counter as his sister sneezed again. "Get to bed. I can handle things down here."

She shook her head and looked across the island, where just beyond the closed door, several dogs boarded for the night. Her voice turned melancholy. "Nate hasn't been around all day."

Jax raised his brows in a question.

She shrugged. "Oh, I know he's busy fighting crime and all

that. But he often stops by on his lunch hour or after work, just to check on things. Helps a lot when I have to go to work."

"About that ..."

"Yes?"

He frowned. "Lily, is the dog care place your main line of work?"

Lily sneezed. She grabbed a tissue and blew her nose, all while looking at him with certain curiosity. "You know that I have my own coffee cart, right? That I take it to events and to offices when I'm called?"

"You what?"

"It's the reason I started using Dad's truck. Has a hitch on it."

"This is news to me."

She threw the wadded-up tissue at him, and he ducked reflexively. "You have got to be kidding me. I work multiple jobs, Jax—multiple!" She wagged her head, rolling her eyes. "Pay better attention."

Jax stared back at his sister, her insult filtering through him.

"Oh, don't go getting all lawyer-y on me now."

He scoffed. "Meaning?"

"Standing taller, those cheekbones all chiseled from jaw clenching, and staring me down like I'm in the witness chair or something."

He shrank back from the accusation.

She grabbed another tissue. "You fold easy."

Jax laughed outright now. "Maybe Mom mentioned it?" He shook his head. "Actually, now that I think more about it, I thought Mom said something about you working in that coffee shop on Main Street."

"The Coffee Hole? Please."

He cracked a sideways grin. "The name's terrible, but yes. I

49

saw that place the other day and something about it was familiar."

"That's something, then."

"What is?"

"You had some inkling, so you're not completely empty upstairs when it comes to your family."

Jax crossed his arms, staring after her.

"I suppose you are partially exonerated because I did work at that awful place for a few months." Lily started for the stairs, then stopped and turned around. "Part-time only, but the owner would never take any of my suggestions, so I left. Decided I didn't want to have my name attached to it in any way."

"You do make an excellent cup of coffee."

She nodded. "That I do."

Slowly, Jax began to piece together a picture of what life looked like in Saltwater Beach without him in it. In a flash, he could see his brothers around town, doing their jobs, grabbing lunch with each other, or popping into the family home. He pictured Addi bustling through, her dazzling smile lighting up the room on foggy beach days. In his mind's eye, he even imagined the new hardware store comfortably fading back into its former self.

Until now, it never bothered him to think of living somewhere else, far away from the day-to-day of life in Saltwater Beach. Maybe that's because he hadn't remembered all he had been missing.

Lily continued, breaking into his thoughts. "Getting back to what we were talking about, I miss Nate being around more. Thankfully, Lucky hasn't run off."

Good ol' Lucky. Kind, caring, always around for their mother. A pang of guilt twisted inside Jax. Like Lily, he really didn't know his brother all that well either. He had always thought it was because they were so different. When Jax was out playing catch with buddies, Lucky was in his room building something intricate that would eventually speed across their parents' wooden floors.

Truth was, Lucky was as steady as they came, and Jax had more than once been thankful for his brother and the kindness he had always showed their mother. She spoke of him often— and Lily too—on their video calls.

Lily began stacking clean bowls from the dishwasher when Jax stopped her. "You're fired."

She sneezed again.

He pried her hands off the bowls and turned her around. "Leave now before I send HR after you."

"We wouldn't want that."

"No, we wouldn't. She's mean. Really mean."

"Okay, fine. I'm going to crawl into bed upstairs."

"About that ..."

Lily sniffled and crossed her arms, leaning out one hip. "Yes?"

He knew Lily had a place of her own, but at some point, had moved in here to help their mother. He shifted. "Maybe you'd be more comfortable at home."

"Home?"

"Yes, in your own bed. You do still have your condo, right?"

A strange look flitted across Lily's face, followed by a look so sharp he thought she might stab him with it.

"What did I say now?"

"Can't very well move into a place with some guy living in it."

"Some ... guy?"

"Yes. My renter." Lily rolled her eyes, grabbed another

tissue and sneezed. She wiped her nose. "Mom needed me twenty-four seven, something else you'd have known if you paid better attention."

"She was fine every time I talked to her. Sharp as ever."

"I never said she had dementia. I said she needed me. For the everyday stuff. After a while, it made sense to move in here —for both of us. So I put my things in storage and rented out my place." She sniffled. "I didn't expect to lose her already."

Stunned was an understatement. Jax had spoken often to his mother. Had she mentioned Lily had actually moved in? He wanted to shake his head to loosen up the memories of their conversations stuck in there. Why had he no idea about their living arrangements?

Lily must have sensed his confusion because she smacked him on the shoulder. "Forget about it, darling. We all know what a busy guy you are."

Jax wanted to talk to her—to all of his siblings—about their next steps with the house. But clearly this wasn't the right time to discuss all that, especially with him so much in the dark about, well, everything.

Instead, with a slight shake of his head, he changed the subject, hoping to keep her from exerting herself any more than she already had. "Just go on to bed and don't worry about Chase. You know how he is."

"No, I don't. How is he?"

Silence fell between them. He could have left that last statement out. How could he explain Chase's behavior toward him when he didn't understand it himself? The last time they talked was after he announced his wedding was off. Instead of sympathy, Chase had sneered a one word reply: "Figures."

He'd wracked his brain, trying to figure out when Chase changed from the happy-go-lucky teen with a bent toward long-distance running and late-night sneak attacks on his brothers to an oft-disgruntled adult.

He didn't know the answer, unfortunately.

"I'm not trying to alarm you. Listen, I'm sorry that I haven't been doing more to find him. My thoughts are that he wants to be alone to grieve Mom in his own way, but maybe you're right. We need to show him that we're putting forth the effort to find him." He paused. "Is it possible he would have taken a gig at another port?"

"It's crossed my mind, though he told me just last week that he plans to stay here for as long as he can afford to."

They watched each other in silence for a moment before Jax said, "Go on up to bed. Do you have everything you need?"

Lily nodded, her eyes watery. "I'm good." On her way up the stairs, she called back down to him. "Get Addi to help you close things up after the last pup leaves for the day."

Jax nodded, though only to placate her. He and Addi had fallen into a decent rhythm of polite conversing whenever they ran into each other at the house. Some might say they had gone beyond the surface with the occasional reference to times in their past.

But never anything particularly deep, though he had been tempted. Still, with his plans to leave sooner rather than later, he wouldn't mind keeping it that way. No sense upending her plans or his.

Jax wandered around the kitchen, inspecting the walls, the outlets, anything that might need some TLC before they made a final decision of what to do with the place. He could feel Addi's presence even before she announced she had walked into the room.

"Hey," she said. "Have you seen Lily?"

Olive pushed her way through the door right then,

53

wagging her bushy tail. She hopped up and put both front paws on Jax's leg. He glanced down at her. "Mighty forward of you, missy."

Addi laughed and stepped closer, gently telling Olive, "Off, girl."

Jax stopped Addi with a light touch of her arm. Their eyes met and held. After a day inside that pen, she should have smelled of earth and animal, but all he took in was jasmine, like the kind that grew along just about every fence in town.

Her eyes flickered to his mouth, but snapped upward again.

"She's fine."

"She?"

He grinned. "Olive. I wouldn't mind if she hung around with me this afternoon while I work."

A smile grew on her face. "Oh, really?"

"Don't look so shocked."

"It's difficult not to be."

"You think I'm an ogre or something?"

Her smile dimmed, and it was almost as if he could see the movement of questions in her mind as they played across her face. She must have chased them away, because her expression brightened. She took a step back then, breaking the tension between them.

"Well, I'm very glad to see you two have become friends."

Jax bent down to acknowledge Olive. It also gave him a chance to break eye contact with Addi and collect his thoughts. Dangerous thoughts.

"So," she said, breaking back into his musings, "Lily?"

He stood up and leaned his bum against the counter. "Right. She's sick, so I sent her to bed."

"Oh, no. I'm sorry. I was just going to ask her if she had more dog food somewhere, but—"

"Not to worry." He strode over to the pantry and dragged out the massive bag. "Where would you like this?"

She held up the plastic container in her hand. "I'll fill this up, and it should be good for tomorrow."

"I don't suppose you could stay until closing time tonight?"

She frowned. "I'm so sorry, but I can't. I, uh, have other plans."

As in, you're headed out to meet some guy? He wanted to throw a punch at his own chin for letting that thought come to him.

Instead, he simply nodded. "Lucky and I'll be fine. And hopefully Lily will be back at it tomorrow."

"I'm really very sorry I can't stay and help, Jax."

After she left, Jax began cleaning up his mess, thoughts about Addi playing with his heart. This softening within him was ... unusual. He ran a hand through his hair, lingering halfway between doing the job of cleaning up and thinking back to earlier days. She was no longer the girl he'd hung out with, that's for sure. But if he were honest, he had noticed her in a different light even back then, before he had run off to follow his dreams.

Olive shifted, reminding him of the tasks at hand. He wiped away the putty shavings dotting the floor when a random thought struck him: Could he ever come back to Saltwater Beach to stay?

The answer was easy: no. Absolutely not. Even his mother had told him to spread his wings and live the big city life he'd always dreamed about.

Now his life's plans were set in motion. Despite this

detour, he was still on the fast track to becoming partner with a national firm—even slightly ahead of the schedule he had laid out for himself. How many thirty-somethings could say that?

He nodded, though only Olive was around to see it. *Stay on track, don't veer.* His fallback mantra ran through his head. He continued with his chores, putting everything in a safe place so he could find it all again tomorrow.

Olive followed him around, the sound of her breathing the only outward sign of her presence, as if she were trying to be polite and not disturb him.

He glanced at her several times as she kept close. His heart gripped whenever he'd notice the place where one eye was missing. It didn't seem to bother her though. But maybe that's why she kept so close to him, her movements nearly mirroring his.

Lucky was mopping a pen as three dogs watched. He stopped mid-mop, pushed his glasses up his nose, and cracked a smile. "I see you have a companion."

"She's in love with me. What can I say?"

He went back to mopping, still smiling. "Guess you're one lucky guy, then."

"Glad I ran into you. Have you seen Nate around today?"

He shook his head. "Nope."

"Are you okay? Concerned about Chase?"

He shrugged. "I was at first, but the more I thought about it—not really. He's kind of a loner ..." Lucky looked up. "Don't say it."

Jax chuckled. "Say what?"

"You think I'm a loner too. But that's not what I meant."

"What I think is that you're a lot like Mom in that you prefer animals to humans. Coming from the things I see and hear daily at work, I can't blame you."

Lucky stopped again. "Probably one of the nicest things

you've said to me, big brother." He was quiet a moment. "You thinking of sticking around a while longer?"

There was that idea again, but no ... impossible. Especially with his chance at partnership as close as a phone call. Instinctively, he put his hand to his pocket where he kept his phone. It would be embarrassing to voice this, but Mom's passing couldn't have come at a worse time for him. Jax shook his head. "Sorry, no."

Lucky nodded once and went back to his sweeping.

"But Lily's sick, so I'll stick around a little longer." Jax paused, watching his brother putter. "I can get some work done from here and help run this place until she's well enough. Speaking of which, what can I do to help you finish up tonight?"

"Nothing, really." A German shepherd with a rope in his mouth bumped his brother's leg. Without looking, Lucky grabbed the end of the rope and tugged. The dog tugged back. "These three will be heading home soon. It's only Olive who will need to be fed and walked later."

Olive let out a whine of acknowledgement and sat without being told. Jax reached down and patted her head. "Guess it's you and me, kid."

Lucky straightened suddenly. "There is one thing you could do, if you don't mind. We need a closer for that screen door back there. Can you stop at Barrett's this evening?"

Jax gulped. And have another encounter with Vic? Not a chance ... then again, maybe it was time to show the old-timer he was no longer the incorrigible teen of his old nemesis.

"Sure. I'll take Olive with me." He winked at Lucky. "To run interference."

Chapter Four

A ddi missed the feelings these long summer days once evoked. As a teen, the sun's glow meant staying out later and sleeping in too. She closed her eyes and breathed in, as if doing so would remind her of those salty-air days from the past, but instead, all she smelled was metal. She counted out the last of the small tension springs her father had asked her to restock and pushed herself up from the floor.

Her hands felt greasy to the touch, so she grabbed a rag from the counter and did her best to wipe away the grime in time for the next customer to walk in. She promised her father she would keep the place open for him while he ... rested.

The bell on the front door chimed, and Addi put a smile on her face.

"Hello, again."

"Jax?" She glanced down toward the floor where a commotion was taking place. "Well, hello there, Olive."

The dog's tail wagged furiously. The happy pup jumped up until her paws landed on the counter, where she held on, peering at Addi.

Addi laughed and petted her head. "Such a pretty girl." She looked at Jax as lightly as possible. "What are you doing here? More putty?"

"Nope. Came for one of these." He held up the busted item. "You call it a closer, right?"

"Actually, Dad calls those a hold open." She laughed again. "But same difference. I'll find one for you."

She retrieved one from a display rack behind her and slid it across the counter. "Anything else?"

He seemed momentarily tongue tied. Finally, "I didn't see your car out front. Is this where you were headed when you left the house?"

She hesitated, breaking eye contact with him. "Yes. So, my father wasn't feeling well and asked me to cover until closing, which is coming up"—she glanced at the clock on the wall—"pretty soon here."

"Glad I caught you then."

"Hm. Me too. This is for the screen door out back, right?"

"Bingo." He was glancing around now. "As you know, I ran into your father the other day when I was in here buying paint. I wasn't aware you worked here too. You're a busy woman."

She shrugged. What else could she add? Jax wasn't aware of much of anything in her life, so why would he know she spent almost as much time in this hardware store as she did in his mother's home?

Everything about this moment felt surreal. One part of her wanted to take him by the hand and fill him in on everything he had missed. The other part? When she thought further about the things that had laid comfortably buried for the past twelve years, she found herself wishing that he would simply go back to Chicago.

Yet her heart dropped at the thought.

Jax's brows dipped, and he watched her intently. "Are you feeling all right?"

She quirked a smile at him. She was good at mustering up when she needed it. "Sure am."

He eyed her. "You didn't walk here, did you?"

Addi sighed and began busying herself with ringing up Jax's order. The best thing that could happen right now would be a new customer—or two or three—would walk right in through that front door and cause her to be instantly occupied.

When she looked up, Jax's head was tilted to one side. "Addi?"

Right. He'd asked her a question. "I usually take my bike to the shop—it's an easy ride from my home." She casually looked at him. "But I wasn't expecting to be in here today, so I didn't have it with me at your house."

"Because you walked to the daycare."

"Mm-hm." She gave him the total of his purchase and put the item into a bag. Would it be too obvious if she were to start drumming her fingers on top of the counter?

Jax dug out a couple of bills and placed them in front of her. Then he glanced at Olive, who had been sitting like a perfect angel next to him. "It's settled then."

Addi took the money and slid it into the cash register drawer. "What is?"

"We're giving you a ride home."

She waved both hands like fans in front of her. "No, really. I'll be fine. Really." She gestured toward the glass door, trying not to notice its desperate need for a good cleaning. "There will still be about an hour of daylight by the time I'm out of here."

Olive let out a whine. Jax frowned and tilted his head again. "She sounds disappointed."

Addi cracked up.

His dark eyes watched her. "Seriously, Addi. This had to have been a two-mile walk. Let Olive and I drop you at home. We'll wait right over there in the toy aisle until you're done closing up."

He had her laughing again.

Addi had always loved Jax's voice, even when they were young, and the way he lowered it now made her knees want to buckle right there behind her father's counter. "It's the least we could do." His eyes zeroed in on hers. "For someone who helped my mother so often."

Oh. Of course that's what he meant. This altruism had everything to do with remembering his sweet mama and nothing to do with personal feelings for her at all. Sure-sure-sure.

Eventually, Addi turned up both hands. "Okay. Good deal. I'll just be a few minutes."

Her apartment sat two-and-a-quarter miles from the store, and once they arrived, Addi admitted to herself she wasn't sorry she had accepted a ride from Jax. She forced back a yawn. Then her stomach grumbled.

Jax chuckled. "Guess I'd better get Olive back for her dinner too."

"You haven't fed her yet?"

"Sorry, no. But, hey, I'm new at this. Remember?"

"My goodness." She hopped out of his father's old truck and waved him in. "Come on. I'll feed you both." When he didn't move, she peered at him through the open window. "It's the least I can do, for the ride, I mean."

He gave her a congenial nod and hopped out to follow her, Olive following along behind him.

* * *

The inside of Addi's apartment looked exactly as he might have imagined. Warm, soft, lavishly ... feminine. The entire place was painted shades of white—even the vaulted ceiling and the bricks around her fireplace. The flooring, though, was well-worn wood stained dark.

Olive pranced into the kitchen and sat. It didn't take long for Addi to fish a treat out of a bag in her cupboard then heap praise on the pup for sitting so well.

Oh, to be a dog.

Treat in her mouth, Olive trotted over to the fireplace and curled up on a sheepskin rug.

"Are you okay with her laying on that?"

"Of course." Addi flashed a smile. "She's a love. How could I say no to her?"

"How indeed." He glanced around the room, noting the family photo with Addi and her parents, a painting of a garden fully in bloom, and a simple black-and-white sketch of the Eiffel Tower.

Addi moved deftly through her kitchen, retrieving pans and a wooden cutting board. He pulled his gaze away from her bare feet and instead let it alight on the fireplace, edged with tiny white lights. "Do you use your fireplace much during the cold months?"

Addi giggled.

"What?"

She leaned across the island. "Let me tell you a secret—it's fake."

He whipped another look at it, then stepped across the room for a closer inspection. Sure enough. It wasn't attached to anything. His father, the contractor-slash-investor-slash-surfer, would be horrified he hadn't immediately spotted that.

A pang of grief struck him, remembering his dad's bold

laughter. He'd made a good life for them, but done it on his terms, which included quiet early mornings alone with his board. His father had hung up his surfboard abruptly, which had surprised Jax, though he had to admit—he was preoccupied with school and his early adult years so he hadn't questioned it much.

They'd lost him not too long after that.

Jax chased away his sudden memories. When he turned back around, a charcuterie board laden with chunks of cheese, sliced salami, olives, and nuts had appeared on the island, and she was dumping some kind of pasta into a large sauté pan.

"Leftovers," she said. "Good ones, though. Hope you don't mind."

"Me? Of course not. It smells delicious."

Addi opened an upper cabinet door. "Would you like a glass of wine?"

"Sure. If you're having some."

She smiled. "Pasta almost requires it, don't you think?"

"So," he said after she'd handed him a glass of red wine, "about the fake fireplace."

She shrugged a shoulder. "I always wanted a fireplace growing up, but our house didn't have one."

"So you made sure that a place of your own would."

"Yes. Believe me, I tried to find an apartment or house I could afford that had its own fireplace. None of the apartments in my price range do, though, so—voila—I ordered this online." She held out her glass. "Cheers."

He sipped his wine. His penthouse rental back home had plenty of white and black, some wood accents, and tons of glass. Mainly, because that's what Mara preferred, and she had helped him choose the place. Unlike his father, who paid attention to such details, he was too busy with his caseload to spend time choosing paint colors. So after obtaining the landlord's approval, he had handed her his credit card and told her to have at it.

Which she did.

When Addi turned back to whatever was bubbling in the pan on her stovetop, Jax wandered back in front of that fireplace. He had hardly used the real one in his place, maybe once with Mara on a cool night, but otherwise, never.

"Here." Addi wandered into the room and flipped a switch. The fake fireplace lit up immediately. "Isn't that the coolest? It doesn't give off much heat, but it's the ambience I was going for anyway."

He jerked a look at her, a memory coming into view.

"What is it?"

"What is what?"

"You had a funny look on your face just now."

"Oh, that. My mind wandered to the past." He crossed his arms, still holding the glass of wine. "It's been doing that a lot lately."

"Well, sure." Her voice softened. "You only lost your mother a couple of weeks ago. I'm afraid to tell you, but you'll be doing that on and off for some time to come."

"Hm. Yes. Though I don't recall doing it so much after my father died. Of course, I was a bone-headed college student at the time. Can't say I was too aware of what was going on outside of the bubble I walked around in."

She wandered back to the kitchen as he continued to look around the room. He asked, "You've been to Paris?"

"Never."

"The sketch is signed by a name that looks French." He shrugged. "Thought perhaps you had picked it up on a stroll along Ponts des Arts."

65

"Well, it's a lovely thought anyway."

"And you like to read." He'd stated it plainly, as the wall to the right of her fireplace was lined with books. He looked more closely. "Cookbooks. You like to read ... cookbooks?"

She laughed. "Among other things, yes."

Jax whistled, which caught Olive's attention. "Sorry, girl. It's just ... so much paper on one wall."

"You're a lawyer though. Aren't you inundated with paper?"

"Precisely. Which is why I rarely read paperbacks anymore."

"No time to read?"

"Not much, but when I do, I use my e-reader."

Addi gasped. "Then how do you make notes and dog-ear the pages?"

"I don't. I just read for enjoyment."

She brought the charcuterie board over to a small coffee table. "Well, there's something we can agree on."

He chuckled. "Didn't realize we were sparring."

She smiled. "We're not. Anyway, I just gave the pasta a stir and turned off the stovetop so we could sit here for a few minutes by the, um, fire. Okay with you?"

"Of course."

With the dog at his feet, the flames of the fake fire licking the air, and Addi sitting next to him on the couch less than an arm's length away, he couldn't help but hear the words *what if* pounding in his head.

"So." Addi sat back, cradling her wine. "Getting back to our earlier discussion. What was the memory that caught you off guard, if you don't mind me asking?"

"Your use of the word *ambience*."

She let loose an incredulous laugh.

He turned to look fully at her. "It stuck out to me because you used that word the last time we went to the fair, before I left for college." He didn't add that it was the same night she had won him a teddy bear. And that she'd kissed him, sending his head and heart spinning right out of the friendship zone. He wondered if she even remembered all that.

"Really now."

The air crackled between them. "Perfectly serious here."

She paused. "Well, what's not to love about the night air filled with the stench—er, the aroma of burned kettle corn and carnies who had worked for twelve hours straight?"

He chuckled at that, acknowledging the break in the tension. Yet he still could not take his eyes off her. Addi was every bit as lovely now as when she was a teenager, when he found himself falling for her. He barely remembered being angry with her later that summer—how had he allowed that to happen?

Her expression had gone pensive. "For the record, I remember that night. It was your last time at the fair before college."

He shot her a look, suddenly remembering, once again, what had caused him to seethe. "And before you announced your engagement to what's-his-name."

She gave her head a little shake, tearing her gaze from his. "I have an idea. Let's not talk about anything after that night. Deal?"

Instinctively, he knew she was right to suggest that. Everything changed in their friendship after that night. He couldn't attribute the slide away from each other to any one thing, and never could. Instead, it always had felt to him like a slow and painful fade to black. The next thing he remembered she was engaged to someone he never thought worthy of her.

He took a sip of wine, buying him time, watching her over his glass. A palpable tension in his head dared him to reach out and touch her silky skin, but he forced it into submission. He would not be revisiting the past anytime soon, because that would only serve to reopen old wounds. The last thing he needed was to limp home to Chicago, acutely injured.

Still, as he sat there on the couch, holding off a desire that had both surprised him with its ferocity as well as its familiarity, he realized that, at this moment, he had more questions than answers.

Chapter Five

They had moved into dangerous territory. Addi sensed Jax knew it too. She could have predicted this would happen the moment she peered back into the truck and invited him in. She chalked up that lapse in judgment to having an out-of-body experience, one that failed to connect with her brain. In reality, from the minute Jax stepped into her home, warning bells had been going off in said brain, and she had been trying to find the off switch ever since.

The more Jax made himself comfortable, the more he connected with her life and memories inside her home, the more she felt herself pushing hard at the barriers she had erected on day one of their reunion.

But what good would it do to start something that they couldn't finish? To allow herself to think of this man, this long-lost friend, as anything other than exactly that?

Addi placed her glass of wine on the table, skillfully sliding farther away from Jax as she did. She had so many questions about his life, but every time she formed a thought in her head, she feared it would connect them to the distant past—a past that she no longer cared to think or speak about again.

Even more, she didn't care to talk to Jax about herself. For one, she lived a rather boring life that would take all of thirty seconds to explain. Unless she found herself in the weeds of history, of course, which might take a machete to slash her way out of.

She refocused her gaze on Jax, still too close to her, her mind flipping back to the boy he once was, yet keenly mindful of the man he had become. His eyes had darkened the moment she blurted out that she would rather not talk about "that night." The tension between them had tightened. He had been about to kiss her, she just knew it. Oh, how she wanted that ...

But she couldn't allow it. Would not.

"Anyway," she said, sitting back against the couch as forcefully as she could, "tell me about your life in Chicago. You always talked about leaving this one-horse beach town and living the big city life. Is it everything you hoped for?"

He blinked. "I—yes. It is."

"Good." That's what she had expected, so why did his answer make her feel so disappointed?

He, too, sat back against the couch. A sign of solidarity? More likely it was because she had torpedoed their conversation. He put his arm up on top of the cushions behind them and offered her a slight smile, surprising her. "I'm with a national firm now, handling cases I never thought possible at this point of my career."

"Sounds gratifying."

"It is." He pressed his lips together a moment, considering her. "I haven't said anything to my family about this, but I've been waiting for a call. If all goes as planned, I will be made a partner, well, a junior partner in the firm soon."

REUNION IN SALTWATER BEACH

"Wow—that's great news, right? I mean, it sounds like huge news for someone so young. Congratulations, Jax."

He lapsed into the boy she remembered. Soft, almost-shy smile, eyes that danced, mouth appearing tongue-tied. Once again, the years faded away.

Jax cleared his throat. "You're right. I would be the youngest partner in the firm." He shifted. "If it happens. Nothing's set in stone, of course."

"It'll happen."

Quiet fell between them. Olive stirred on the sheepskin rug. He took another sip and zeroed in on her. "How about you, Addi? Do you have aspirations outside of Saltwater?"

"No. My life is here."

He seemed to weigh that. "But you could go to college? Travel?"

"Go back to college at thirty-one?"

"Why not?"

She shifted. "Not all of us have the same career goals as you."

"I didn't mean to imply there was anything wrong with the work you do."

"If it sounds more impressive, you might like to hear that I earned my culinary certificate from SC."

"Saltwater College?"

She nodded.

"Congratulations. That's amazing news. Have you been able to put it to use here?"

"Somewhat." She sipped her wine. "I've done a bit of commercial baking, mainly for Lily's coffee cart business."

"Something else I wasn't aware of."

She leaned her head to the side. "I'm sorry."

He shook his head. "I was musing out loud."

"Hold on a moment, would you?" Addi leapt off the couch and took the few steps into the kitchen. "I want to give the pasta a stir and make sure it's still hot enough."

"Would you like me to join you at the counter?"

She hesitated for a beat. "Sure. But would you mind taking Olive out for a quick pit stop first?" Having him leave, even if only for a moment, would buy her the time she needed to regroup.

While they were gone, Addi gulped several deep breaths. What was she doing with this man in her apartment? Had she lost all her good sense? Inviting him over for dinner like they're a, a couple!

She glanced at the door, hoping he would change his mind about returning. Was that too much to ask? Addi rolled her eyes at her own thoughts. Of course, he would be back—probably looking all windblown and delicious.

She added a brief jolt of heat to the pasta dish before plating it, reminding herself that Jax was fully ensconced in his life in Chicago. It hadn't surprised her that he had found success there, even though a small part of her wondered if spending more time here in Saltwater could have a luring effect on him.

Then again, with his mother gone, why would it?

When they returned, she slid a small bowl of kibble laced with some broth under Olive's nose before directing Jax to sit on a stool at the counter.

"This smells delicious."

"Thank you. Now, eat before it gets cold."

"Yes, dear."

She jerked a look up at him, her heart picking up the pace. Her mother used to say the very same thing to her father whenever they were in the middle of terse words. But Jax was giving her a good-natured smile.

She erased her preconceived thoughts and sat next to him. Everything about this felt normal and comfortable, instead of temporary. She searched for a way to keep the topic off her. What should she bring up? Movies? The weather? If he had ever played pickleball?

She twirled some pasta with her fork, happy the conversation no longer focused on her. "You told me about your work in the big city, but how about your life there? What's that like?"

"Hmm. Great question. Let me think about how to answer that."

"I mean, you've got the arts, the river, the baseball ..."

"And the work. Mountains of it."

"Right. But I'm sure you unwind sometimes. At least on weekends."

He wore a doubtful expression.

"Staycation, at least?"

Finally, he broke his silence. "This trip to Saltwater is the only vacation I've had in several years."

Addi stared at him, her fork hovering above her plate. She had been so mesmerized by sitting this close to her onetime flame that she had missed the signs of wear on his face. Crow's feet deeper than her other thirty-something friends, slight darkening beneath his eyes—the signs had been there all along. Until now, she might have attributed them to the death of his only living parent. But overwork could make those kinds of marks on a life too.

"That's not good."

He speared a chunk of chicken with his fork and sliced the air with it, a challenge in his eyes. "I take it you travel often?"

"I go on long walks along the beach whenever I can." She could play this game. "Why would I want to travel anywhere when I live in such a beautiful place? I mean, even the traffic is light except for summer."

He leaned closer, his hand grazing hers as it rested on the island. "That's not what I was asking." A ripple of surprise scurried through her, landing at the base of her throat. Here he went again, awakening her senses, rendering her momentarily unable to respond.

He continued, his voice low, those eyes penetrating. "Why didn't you marry what's-his-name?"

She inhaled, getting her bearings. Simple answers were the best way to shut down a conversation. At least she hoped that was true. "Bradford and I weren't right for each other."

His gaze lingered on her face, dropped briefly to her mouth, then rolled back up again to greet her eyes. "I could have told you that."

"I believe you took care of that years ago." She was moving dangerously close to the memories from his last summer here, when he expressed his opinion she was making a mistake. She swallowed and turned the conversation to him. "There's no ring on your finger either."

He raised an eyebrow but didn't reply.

"Heard you were engaged." She kept her voice casual.

"Did you now?"

She wouldn't be intimidated. "What happened there?"

He leaned toward her, resting his arms on his knees, the shape of his lips familiar in a new and treacherous way. "I'll tell you if you tell me."

She didn't believe him, not for one short second, but did she shrink back? Move away? Scoot over?

No. She leaned in closer, an invisible pulley tugging her

past the point of levelheadedness. There was no good reason to let this go any further. A secret still hung between them, one she conveniently pushed to the back of her mind.

Plus, he would be leaving Saltwater Beach for good soon, something she continued to turn over in her mind ad nauseam. Without his mother here to visit, Jax's occasional visits would transform into almost never.

Again, there was zero reason to allow this ... whatever this was ... to continue. "Ja—"

"Ad—"

Silence, followed by a certain headiness that was becoming more and more difficult to deny. He had taunted her with his presence, and she had no other defenses to offer him. Jax's fingers tangled with hers, warm to the touch. She sucked in a breath, her eyes fluttering upward to find him staring back at her with the kind of desire she had dreamed about for too long to admit.

He touched her cheek with his other hand and leaned toward her until—a wet nose made an appearance between them, followed by a whine, then two paws landing on Addi's leg.

Olive!

Addi giggled. Jax pulled back sharply. Olive stood on her hind legs beneath the island overhang, panting furiously while looking from Addi to Jax and back again.

Addi jumped to her feet. She would get them both a glass of water—yes, that's what she would do. Jax turned his attention to petting the animal with the not-so-perfect (or maybe very perfect?) timing. And suddenly the tilt-a-whirl they had both been gripping straightened and slowed to a halt.

As she was filling the second glass, Addi sneaked another

look at Jax. He kept his focus on the beautiful Olive. Well, *fine*. Maybe that was for the best.

Addi turned off the spigot and carried the glasses of water over to the island, all the while fighting a tinge of resentment aimed at the one-eyed dog who so obviously had captured Jax Cooper's heart.

* * *

Several days had gone by, along with a dozen phone calls, but Jax hadn't forgotten that dinner with Addi. Her gentleness, that half-smile she still gave him when she was thinking about something ... the way she padded around her apartment in bare feet. Jax blew out a breath and swiped a hand over his bedhead. He would have to thank Olive for saving him from doing something that night he might have regretted days later.

Thankfully, their conversation fell back into polite step after their near ... connection. He had thanked her for dinner, then taken Olive home. And that was that.

Jax had been working remotely ever since from the room he once shared with a mix of his brothers when they were all young. But after hours with his legs folded beneath the same desk he had used to practice his cursive, Jax had begun to pace, his phone stuck to his ear, as he made call after call, discussing settlements and potential trial dates, among other things.

The only call he had yet to receive was the one regarding his future at the firm.

The hacking sounds of Lily coughing in the next room interrupted his preoccupation with the Burger case file on the desk—and the fact that he didn't know how long the firm would allow him the freedom to work from his childhood bedroom in California.

"Jax!"

He winced. The cough might be real, but Lily was regaining her energy. Her frenetic brain showed signs of revving up again, bit by bit. He overheard her spitting out a to-do list to Lucky that made him wish he hadn't agreed to stay. Or at least to stay *here*.

Something twisted in his gut when he thought about the day he would board a plane home for Chicago. It was coming soon. It had to be. Why, after all these years, would he give staying longer in Saltwater even a passing thought?

"Jax! He posted! Chase posted!"

Jax swung open his sister's door to find her sitting up in bed, a pile of wadded up tissues surrounding her. Lily's eyes, though red-ringed, lit up for the first time since he had arrived.

"Chase posted on Facebook!" She held up her iPad. "He's not dead."

"Who said anything about being dead?" Jax strode over. "Let me see."

She held up her hand and shrunk back. "Get away from me or you'll get sick too!"

He backed off. "Fine." He ran his thumbs over his phone, searched for the social media app, and clicked.

"Do you see it?"

"Not yet."

She clucked her tongue. "What's taking you so long?"

He looked up. "Reinstalling the app."

"Jax!" She screwed up her face.

"What can I say, Lily?" He shrugged. "I'm a very busy man. Besides, who uses Facebook anymore?"

She rolled her eyes. "You sound just like Chase. He hardly uses it anymore, either, but kept his account for Mom—she wanted him to post photos from the boat." Lily tossed her iPad to the end of the bed. "There. See?"

He ran his gaze over the post. "Is that it?"

"It's something!"

"It says, 'Your sin will find you out.'"

She lunged for her iPad and sat back. "I know what it says! Oh, I'm so relieved. Aren't you?"

Jax thought about that. Relieved? His brother disappeared before they laid their mother to rest. Now he posts a cryptic quote on his Facebook page. "I believe the word I'm looking for is baffled. What does it mean?"

Lily sighed. She grabbed another tissue and blew her nose into it. "It's a Bible verse, in case you'd like to crack one open again one of these days. The Israelites were being told to subdue the land—or else. Something like that."

"I meant, what does it mean to Chase? Why do you think he posted it?"

"How should I know? I'm only the sister who no one ever pays any attention to."

"Martyr."

"Ingrate."

Jax wagged his head at his sister and scrolled through his contacts. He found Chase's name and hit the call button, but it went straight to voicemail. He caught eyes with her. "Phone's still off."

"Yeah." Lily's voice sounded melancholy.

"But at least we know he's not dead." Jax gave his sister a wink. "Listen, I'm going to take a break from work now and look at Mom's estate. I'd like to see the books for the daycare, too. Are you ready to talk about what you'd like to do with the place now?"

"The place?"

"Yes." He gestured with his hand around the room. "The house, the business, car, et cetera."

She dabbed her eyes with a tissue, and he wasn't sure if it was because of her cold or another emotion. "I suppose so. You're leaving soon, aren't you?"

"I have to."

"Do you?"

Lily stared at him, a vague look of pleading in her eyes. To him, she never seemed to be the overly nurturing type. Dramatic, yes. Caring—absolutely. But her emotions, the kind that showered small children with flowing words, were mostly kept to herself.

Instead, Lily was a doer. If he had to choose her love language—his mother loved to talk about that—he would say acts of service. Yes, his sister liked to do unto others.

Which is probably why she was so worried about Chase. She could not fix whatever had spooked him. Truth was, neither could he. No one could help Chase until he was willing to tell them all why he was running.

Jax suspected his sister wanted him to stay until then, but that was an impossibility. "I'll stay as long as I'm able," he said, finally. "At least until we make some decisions and get Mom's estate squared away."

"Thanks. Mom wrote everything down in a stack of ledgers in her office." She nodded toward the hall. "She loved to sit in that writing desk near the window and let the ocean breezes in while she worked."

"More like fretted."

Lily smiled, though her eyes were downcast. "Yeah."

Jax took the stack of ledgers to the porch out front, where a couple of rocking chairs gently aged in the salt air. He had been warned by his superiors in Chicago not to allow his office's rare water view keep him from getting all his billable hours in. But how many times had he run out of his childhood home's front door, past these welcoming chairs? Had he, even once, sat in them and stared at the sky?

An hour later, Jax wished that instead of focusing on his to-do list, he had stayed focused on that awning of blue over the land. He slapped the last ledger shut as Lucky wandered out, silently slipping into the chair next to his.

A hummingbird hovered nearby, its insistent buzz the only sound between them. Lucky spoke. "It's bad, isn't it?"

"Not hopeless."

"If we sell everything, you mean."

Jax turned toward his little brother, who wasn't so little anymore. He was the only one of them who wore glasses and made t-shirts, shorts, and flip-flops his daily wardrobe. Which wasn't all that unusual for a guy who grew up near the beach.

Maybe Jax and his other brothers were the odd ones.

"The dog care isn't profitable. Doesn't make sense to keep it going, now that Mom isn't here."

Lucky stayed quiet.

"The insurance alone has put it into the red."

"I think ... I think I could turn it around."

Jax smiled, but Lucky only frowned. "Wait. You're serious about that? What about your own aspirations? If I'm not mistaken, you were doing something with computers, right?"

"Apps. I create apps."

"If you didn't have the daycare to worry about, you could finally focus on developing more of your own business."

The screen door opened slowly, Olive pushing against it with her nose, letting herself out. She wandered to the empty space between their chairs, as if convinced they were talking about something that concerned her.

Lucky's hand dropped to Olive's head, idly petting her. "This place has given the dogs of Saltwater a chance to know each other. Their parents too. It's created a community within another."

"That's a nice sentiment."

Lucky scowled.

Jax turned toward him. "If we sell the house, you could take your share and invest it in something you really want. Travel? Employees? A home—"

"I own my condo."

"Yes, of course." Jax's mind searched for the right words to say. He had been born into the role of oldest son, yet felt inadequate to carry out the job as he should. Too much emotion in the mix.

"So you're set on selling our mother's home and closing her business? You think that's what we should do?"

"It's all up for discussion, but I am looking at this from a business standpoint. Like you said, you own your home. So does Lily." Although, he'd recently learned why she continued to stay upstairs in their mother's old room. "And Nate and Chase share theirs. So everyone already has a place of their own."

"Everyone but you."

His little brother leveled a look at him, his eyes surprising him with a taunt. Had never seen that from him before. Jax tried not to dwell on the obscene rent he paid for his penthouse in Chicago. But that was the price of living in the city.

He cleared his throat, intent on keeping this conversation from degrading into an argument. Mom had made him the executor of her will, and no one else seemed interested in digging through the details of what she had left behind on this earth. So he had taken it upon himself. Why did that suddenly make him the target?

"Naturally," he continued, "with the sale of the house, the business would go too. But I propose we end it now." When Lucky glared at him, he asked, "Is there any reason not to?"

Lucky stood and stepped off the porch. He turned around, his arms spread wide. "I could give you several, but you won't listen. You never have."

Jax watched his brother stalk off while questions ran through his mind. How did this become about him? When had Lucky said anything to Jax that he hadn't listened to?

The screen door squeaked open again and Addi stepped onto the porch. The wooden slats whined as she stepped softly toward the rocking chair Lucky had vacated. But instead of taking a seat, she stood with folded arms and looked out toward the west.

He tried to decipher the meaning behind her intensity. One thing was for certain, he was beginning to get used to seeing her every day around here and wasn't looking forward to the day when that would end. "Something on your mind?"

She waited a beat before turning her gaze on him. "You always seem so ready to just walk away."

His shoulders slumped, and he blew out a long breath, deflating.

"I'm right, aren't I?"

His back stiffened against the chair, and he shut his eyes. Where had this come from all of a sudden? Had she been eavesdropping? Would it matter if she had? Jax opened both hands in surrender. "I'm not sure what you're referring to, Addi. Care to tell me?"

She looked at him with clouded eyes. A far cry from the

doe-eyed gaze she had laid on him the other night ... the eyes he had thought about too often ever since.

He turned toward her, continuing. "Because if I've offended you, I want to know about it." His mind immediately shot to that near-kiss the other night at her apartment. If she thought he had changed her mind about wanting to kiss her, well, she was sorely mistaken.

Eventually, she looked away, shaking her head. "I'm sorry, Jax. It's not my place to say anything."

"There is no hierarchy here, just old friends. Say what you have on your mind." When she didn't speak, he leaned toward her. "Addi?"

Regret showed in her eyes before she pulled her gaze away from him. That was the look he had been trying to define earlier. What had brought it on? And why now?

Jax ran a hand down his mug, suddenly realizing he had walked out here in full bedhead mode. He stifled a rueful laugh. Bet Addi was glad their teenaged flirtation hadn't gone any farther.

She frowned. "Were you thinking of something funny?"

Jax raked a hand through his wayward hair and looked at the horizon. "Not exactly. But I guess ... I guess I could have run a brush through my hair before stepping out here."

Addi shifted, her lashes fluttering. She rolled her gaze up to his mop of hair, a slight smile parting her lips.

"Yeah, you find it funny too. Admit it." Beside him, Olive whined and headbutted his calf. He swallowed and reached out to pet her, which caused the canine to burrow hard into his hand. He experienced the slow release of tension and the real possibility that his blood pressure was sinking back into the safe zone. Was this what his mother felt when surrounded by animals?

Jax pictured her sitting out on this porch, watching dogs romp in the tall grasses of the land surrounding their home. Maybe he hadn't slowed down enough to grieve, to think hard about how to handle his family and their emotions at this time in their lives, but frankly, with his caseload and potential partnership, he hadn't had the time.

He glanced at Addi again. She had lived her whole life in Saltwater. Had lost a mother and watched her friends scatter. Perhaps this silence from her was her way of expressing grief and sadness at seeing the Cooper family home sold and his mother's rather eccentric business closed.

Or ... could he dare to think it had something to do with him leaving Saltwater for good?

He licked away the dryness from his lips. "Chase posted a message online."

"You're kidding." She sat up, gripping the handles of her rocker. "Oh, that's a relief."

"You really were worried about him." Why did that bug him? Surely she and Chase hadn't ever ... dated. Someone would have filled him in about that. Right?

"Well, of course I was. We all have been. He's been missing for days."

Jax frowned, remembering the last time he'd talked to Chase. His brother had gone off half-cocked about how he had to do everything around this place, as if he cared more for their mother than Jax did.

Little did he understand the behind-the-scenes work he had handled for their mother, the late-night calls they had shared when he couldn't sleep (nearly every night) and she wanted to tell him something funny some random dog did.

A pang of melancholy tried to take hold.

"To answer your question, no, I haven't been worrying all

that much about Chase. All along I've believed he needed some time to digest all the change ahead. Quite honestly, Addi, my relationship with Chase has been strained for years. Can't say I understand why that is or how it happened."

She turned to him, her eyes searching his face.

He continued. "It's silly, but the bad blood between us seems to have happened around the time I went away to college. I thought maybe he was mad at me."

"Kind of a long time to stay mad at someone." Her words came softly.

"Like I said, I knew it was silly." He leaned his head against the back of the chair and sighed. He couldn't bring himself to ask Addi about her relationship with Chase. Maybe he didn't want to know. "Anyway, he'll show himself soon enough— hopefully before I leave Saltwater—and maybe we can finally talk face-to-face about what has been troubling him."

Addi nodded and flashed him a slight smile, as if she were trying to make him feel better. She pushed away from the porch post and turned to leave.

"Did I chase you away?"

"It's not—no. I—I have work to do."

"In other words, it's not me, it's you?"

Addi furrowed her brow. Jax's attempt at a joke obviously landed far off its mark. She bent down and rubbed Olive's head. "C'mon, girl. It's time to go back inside."

Jax touched her hand, and she stilled. "In all seriousness, I appreciate all you've done around here, including when my mother was alive. And I'm sorry I wasn't around more to see it."

She stared into his face, her green eyes searching his.

He whispered, "And you."

"Me?"

Jax reached for her hand, holding it lightly. "I'm sorry I haven't been around more in the last few years to see ... you."

He had not expected those words to cause her eyes to fill with tears like they suddenly had. They were teetering, the two of them, on the precipice of something he didn't understand. One minute she was the Addi of his youth, smiling wide and making quips. The next, she grew quiet and introspective, almost shy.

Either way, she was beautiful and unforgettable. And he was the stupidest guy for leaving Saltwater before ever telling her so.

Chapter Six

"I'm so glad you suggested this." Lily pulled several cupcake pans out of the cabinet and slid them onto the counter.

Addi plunked a roll of parchment paper next to them, along with avocados and cacao powder. "I've been wanting to try some new things, and with summertime here, I thought this would be a good time."

"Well, I, for one, am glad to see it." Lily looked Addi in the eye. "You're always so generous."

"Stop."

"I'm serious! One of these days you should bake some of this stuff just for yourself—a treat for Addi-girl."

"And add an extra hundred pounds to this bod? No thanks." Addi laughed. "I'm so glad you're feeling better now. This'll be fun."

"And goodness knows we could use some fun around here. Speaking of fun, have you seen Jax today?"

"Interesting segue. How is that speaking of fun?" Addi been trying not to think too hard about Jax and her negative reaction to him out on the porch. She had questioned herself thoroughly about that last night, poring over Scripture to get her head on straight.

In the end, it was her pride that had been ruling her. She had wanted him to kiss her that night in her apartment. But he didn't, and she was mad about it. So she took it out on him after his brief discussion with Lucky out there on the porch.

Textbook definition of her reaction. She wasn't proud of it.

Lily wiggled her hand in the air, like a brush off. She did that a lot. "You two almost seemed like you were getting cozy, that's all."

"Cozy? I don't know what you mean."

Lily looked her straight in the eyes. "Oh yes, you do."

Addi slid a large wooden spoon across the counter, along with a look of disdain. "Just follow my directions."

"And keep my opinions to myself?" Lily shot her another look then readied a medium bowl in front of her. She sighed. "I guess I have been rather pointed where you and Jax are concerned, but I can't help myself. I've said it before—I don't want to see your heart broken."

"Uh-huh."

"Or my best friend mad at me for having a dumb brother."

"No problem. Let's get a move on. Start peeling those avos."

"Yes, ma'am."

"And maybe pour me a glass of white wine too."

Lily laughed loudly. "I like this assertive Addi—where'd she come from anyway? Well done."

"Haha—watch out. I might want to mix up extra batches before the night is through."

Jax appeared in the doorway, his phone in one hand. Their

conjoined laughter must have kept them from hearing the clomping of his boots down the stairs.

"Were we disturbing you, big brother?"

He shot his sister a smile that said, *You can't get to me.* "Just wondering about all the frivolity going on around here."

Addi snickered. She caught him glancing too casually at the counter, where cupcakes were cooling. "Can I help you with something?"

"Do you need a taste tester?"

Lily and Addi exchanged a brief glance.

"Oh absolutely. Hold on a second." She took one of the warm cupcakes and lathered it with dark chocolate frosting before handing it to him. "Eat it quick before that frosting melts."

Jax didn't hesitate but swallowed it down in two bites. He licked his finger. "Not usually a cupcake guy, but that's amazing!"

Lily clucked her tongue. "Had no idea you were a health nut, Jax."

He grinned and reached for another. Addi slapped his hand playfully, but when he hesitated, she gestured for him to take it. He wolfed the second one down too.

"Yeah," Jax said after he'd wiped his mouth with a napkin. "I'm all about healthy eating."

"Good." Addi tilted her head. "Because that's vegan, gluten free, and the icing is made with avocado."

He froze. "You're lying."

"Am not."

He shifted, a fake stern look in his eyes, reminding her so much of the old Jax. She used to share the latest gossip with him and give a fake frown. Then he'd shoot back: You're lying. But, of course, she would be proved right all along.

Lily leaned across the counter. "She is ... not."

He looked over at the cupcakes again, assessing them. Addi laughed. "What? Now that you know what's in them, they don't look so appealing anymore?"

"That's not it at all. I'm just wondering why you're not selling these."

She snorted.

"What? I'm not kidding." He put his hands on his slim hips and surveyed the cupcakes. "They're amazingly weird, Addi. Weird sells. Trust me—I've written plenty of contracts."

Lily came around the counter and laid a hand on her brother's shoulder. "Wow. You really know how to woo the girls, don't you? Those are some fine skills you're displaying, big brother."

"To answer your question," Addi broke in, "I'm too busy to start selling cupcakes out of the back of my car, but thank you for the suggestion."

Jax reached for another cupcake, and this time Addi slapped his hand. Their eyes caught, but she quickly looked away. "Those are for the church. Looks like you need some dinner."

Lily cut in. "You've been out of sight for a long time. Have you eaten anything today, Jax?"

"Yes, I have. Two cupcakes."

Lily rolled her eyes. "Such a dumb boy."

Addi snickered again. "I brought over some homemade chicken soup Lily won't eat. You're welcome to it."

"It's not that I won't eat it, honey, it's just that I'm feeling better and want to eat All The Things now. Go for it, Jax. It's in the fridge. Just stay out of our way."

"Well, if you won't share anymore of your cupcakes with me, Addi, then I guess I'll take you up on the soup." Jax pulled the covered dish out of the fridge and warmed a bowl of it up in the microwave. He leaned his behind against the counter and ate a spoonful of the soup, watching the bakers work.

Addi sneaked a look at him, but he caught her gaze and held it, a smile reaching his eyes. "This is fantastic," he said. "Especially loving all the gluten in these noodles."

She licked her lips. "Are you now?"

He took another bite, and she had to control herself from watching his mouth move. Lily shifted, and Addi shot her a look. One look at Lily's goofy expression, and Addi knew she'd been caught. Her face warmed, and she busied herself with filling more cupcake papers with batter.

But she couldn't let Jax's comment go by. Quietly, she said, "It's gluten free."

"What is?"

She looked up. "The soup. Those noodles are not made from wheat flour."

He stopped mid-bite. Lily giggled. Jax's frown deepened. "What are they made from then?"

"Rice." She looked up. "But there are all kinds that can be used. I just like those."

"So our dinner the other night ... at your apartment?"

Lily broke in. "You had dinner at Addi's apartment?" She swung a wild-eyed look at Addi, a sort of *I-warned-you* thing. "You never told me about that."

Addi ignored her. "All of that was gluten free, Jax. You didn't notice, apparently."

A slow grin meandered across his face. "You fooled me. It was all delicious." Jax pushed himself away from the counter. "But what you're telling me is I'm right."

"Right? About?"

"You should open some kind of business—a bakery or restaurant—something."

"I've been telling her that for years," Lily cut in.

"You're much too talented to be wasting it all—"

Addi looked up sharply. "On what? My father? Friends? You think I've wasted my life?" Addi felt the slow release of fun and games being let out of the room. She began to putter again, harshly adding plops of batter into waiting paper cups. What did he know about her life? Or what did Lily really know for that matter?

Silence enveloped her. When Addi raised her head, two sets of eyes were trained on her. Lily's had narrowed slightly, in an analytical way. While Jax's had widened.

He approached her like one might approach a kitten in a corner. "It was meant as a joke, Addi. I just meant you were wasting it on the likes of us. I never meant to imply you have wasted anything about your life."

Tears prickled her eyes. How had this lively evening taken such a downturn? Of course, he didn't mean anything by it. No one ever did. But it hurt, all the same. Because the truth was, she was thirty-one years old and had no plans for the future, other than saving her father and his business from burning to the ground—figuratively—and stepping in to help Lily and Lucky to keep their mother's legacy alive.

Beyond that, she had no idea what else she could do, or even wanted to, for that matter.

As if sensing the tension in the room, Lily bustled about, clattering pans and whisking dirty utensils into the sink. She cleared her throat. "I'm making lasagna for family dinner, Sunday night. Addi, you're invited."

She swiveled a look at her friend. "Me? Don't you have family matters to discuss? I don't want to intrude."

Lily pointed a wooden spoon at her. "You, my bestie, are never an intruder." She gave her brother a resigned look. "Isn't that right, Jax?"

Jax grinned. "Absolutely."

* * *

"You really aren't planning to go to the fair tonight?" Lily's eyes, though a little droopy, widened as if this was big news. It had been a long day of cleaning out closets, preparing to give away some of Melanie's clothing. That and helping Lucky and the teens with some of the more rogue pups that needed extra playtime.

Addi slung her bag over her shoulder and shrugged. "Not this time." She yawned. "I'm looking forward to a hot shower and soft jammies."

"Woohoo, girl. You know how to party."

Addi laughed.

"I guess I'm feeling nostalgic these days." Lily wiped her nose with a tissue. "Wish I wasn't going to miss it."

"Maybe you'll feel well enough by Sunday?" It was Friday, and the fair lasted all weekend long.

"Yeah, I'm fine. Just don't have all my strength back yet." Lily sighed. "It's just that we always went on the first night when we were kids, and later—as you know—as teens. It was always the highlight of the year, a start to summer."

Addi remembered, although it felt like forever since she had been a teen. And except for a few scattered memories, those years weren't all that carefree anyway.

Lily's voice brought her back to the present. "Remember when Mom really wanted to go last year, so we went?" She laughed lightly. "Ate way too much kettle corn, but totally worth it. She loved it."

Addi gave her a side hug. "I remember. You miss her, and I do too."

"Yeah. Maybe I'll go on the last day, when I can really enjoy everything there is to see. Start a new tradition."

Addi smiled. "There you go. Maybe I'll join you."

After they said their goodbyes, Addi headed out to the porch. As she often did, she had walked to work. She usually looked forward to stretching out her legs on the way home, but the fatigue running through her made her question her choice not to drive today.

She hesitated. The other reason she wished she hadn't walked: Her route took her by the park where the fair had been held for the past forty years. Sigh. Lily may have waxed nostalgic about the yearly tradition, but Addi had avoided thinking about it all day. The reason? Because of a memory that had soared into her consciousness ever since Jax rode back into town, causing a nonstop disturbance in her heart.

"It's not my fault."

She exhaled and pushed aside the words, hoping they would just slip away from her memory. Though she could never fully forget who said them and why, the words had laid buried for some time. Until Jax came back to Saltwater, his presence working like a key to unlock old hurts.

And yet ... she felt anything but hurt by the way he looked at her the other night, right on this porch. His eyes held steady on hers, and she would not have been surprised at all if he had kissed her, as he almost did that night at her apartment.

But is that what she wanted? To be taken to the heights that a kiss from Jax Cooper would take her, only to plummet to the depths after he left Saltwater one last time for good?

The spirit was all too willing to fight off desire for her own sanity, but the flesh? Not so much.

One thing the cupcake night debacle taught her, though, is that she had to start moving forward with her life. It was the only way to fully pull her out of the *what ifs* where Jax was concerned. She had started several times to find her purpose, only to allow herself to be yanked backward, as if connected to a giant rubber band.

It was getting old.

The home's front door swung open, and a warm voice spoke. "You weren't planning to say goodnight?"

"I—" She turned, the sound of Jax's voice bringing an instant tremble to her insides.

He stepped out onto the porch, the sight of him like a slow awakening. She hadn't seen him all day, though to be honest, she had flicked multiple glances at the door throughout the day, wondering if he would ever burst through.

Addi blushed, as if Jax could read her mind. Olive bounded out the door behind him. She sat between them as if she were the main attraction.

He laughed and squatted down to pet her.

Addi brushed a quick gaze over the scene. "I guess I'll be going now. Have a good—"

Olive whined and jumped onto her legs to stop her. Addi flashed a look at Jax.

He shrugged. "I didn't put her up to it."

She shook her head and gently told Olive to sit. Then she gave the animal lavish praise. She lifted her gaze to Jax. "Melanie always said she'd never get another dog after losing Chester, but—" She joined Jax in petting Olive's long brown coat, their hands occasionally grazing each other—"how could she resist this little girl? I think if she had lived, she might have eventually adopted her."

"Looks like you're having some trouble with resisting her too."

They were the picture of the perfect couple, weren't they? A man, a woman, and a lovable dog. She bit the inside of her lip, willing herself to stop fantasizing about something that could never be.

"I have a question."

"Ask away." She kept her expression neutral. He probably wanted to ask her any myriad benign questions related to the doggy daycare.

"Would you like to join me for a night of thrills?"

"Would—I, um?"

His deep, resonating laughter chased away the awkwardness. Playfully, he touched her hand. "At the fair tonight. Thought I'd go for old times. Come with me."

She caught the dare in his eyes, like they were fifteen and sixteen again, brainstorming ways to stay out after curfew.

Though she lingered a half second on the thought, ultimately, Addi shook her head. She stood and hitched her purse over her shoulder. "Thank you for the invitation, but I'm beat."

He, too, stood, leaning a sculpted arm against one of the porch covering's low-hanging slats. "Just think about what a spin on the Tilt-a-Whirl would do for your sleepiness." The intimacy of his voice washed over, a tantalizing drawl that nearly made her wobble in place.

"I'd rather not."

He grinned at her, and though carnival-type warning lights went off in her brain, she froze, unable to look away. If she weren't careful, Addi knew she could find herself leaning into the gravity pulling her toward him.

"C'mon. For old time's sake." Jax's gaze continued to hold her there, spellbound. She noticed his Adam's apple bob before he lowered his voice. "I'll be leaving soon, Addi."

And she would never see him again. The mistakes from the past would stay buried, and Addi would go back to the life she had before Melanie's death ushered Jax back home, bringing old memories with him.

Should she stay with her original plan to walk home, slip into jammies, and turn out the lights? Or allow herself this reunion of sorts, spending Friday night at the Saltwater Beach fair with Jax, one of the few places from her childhood where everything felt blissfully ... normal?

She slid another look at him, her heart heavy with indecision. His eyes, dark and pleading, bored into hers. Finally, she relented.

What would it hurt to go?

* * *

If someone put a blindfold over his eyes and plugged his ears, Jax would still know where he was—he could smell the fair for miles. Just as Addi had alluded to the other night when she mentioned the kettle corn smell. She must have forgotten about the burnt churros, though, or how the air became saturated with butter and sweat. Ah, good times.

"What're you smiling about?"

He dipped a look at her cherub face as it peered up at him. "I was just thinking about all those times I beat you at darts."

"Not."

He chuckled. "If I remember, you were quite the competitor." He was relieved his apology the other night had apparently done its job, and she had agreed to come out with him tonight.

"If you mean, I didn't let you win because you're a boy, then guilty."

Jax shrank back, but he couldn't erase the smile from his face. He was eighteen again, on the precipice of his whole future and in love with the prettiest, most adventurous girl in school.

Except he never told her.

Jax had been haunted by that glaring omission over the past few days. To be honest, much longer than that.

Addi gasped. "The swings! I love the swings." She grabbed his hand. "Oh, let's go ride them."

"Thought you were tired."

"I'm getting a second wind!"

"Well, all right then." They chased their way across the uneven grass, dodging little children with sticky hands and strollers overflowing with cheesy game prizes.

Addi jetted ahead of him. She called over her shoulder. "There's no line!"

The carny took their tickets and ushered them through the gate. Jax followed Addi, choosing the swing next to hers.

After they buckled themselves in, she pointed and laughed at something beneath him.

"What?"

"Your feet are cracking me up."

"My ... feet?"

"A grown man—a lawyer!—with his feet dangling from a swing. I love it so much."

He loved this too. Soon the swings began to sway and spin, effortlessly lifting them over the crowd. Burdens were falling away, though he kept himself from naming them all. No sense taking him back to reality when fantasy felt so much better.

The ride spun faster, until they were aloft, high above the fairgoers. The wide smile on Addi's face prodded the long-ignored places inside him, opening his memory bank wider. She flung her arms wide, laughing, and he let his hand reach out to touch hers.

She gripped his fingers, and when he looked at her, the years fell away. He wanted to kiss her. What if he pulled her toward him on this crazy ride? Would they cause a spectacle? Scandalize the children on the chairs around them? Cause a collision?

Most important, would sparks fly?

For him, they already had.

The ride ended, both of them windblown and grinning. Pretty soon, the sun would hide beneath the horizon, and the breezeway clear of young families. Teens would emerge under the moonlight to crowd the fair in packs jostling against one another.

With that in mind, he said, "Let's grab some dinner before the high schoolers get here and eat all the corn dogs."

"Good idea." She bumped him with her shoulder. "I'll take two."

"Again with the competition. All right, all right, I'll take three."

"Hardy-har-har."

They bumped along like this, bantering like kids themselves, while making their way out of the rides corridor toward the food vendors. A carny in front of the basketball dunking game called out, "Win the girl a prize, right here, fella. Show her whatcha got."

He stopped, considering it.

She whispered in his ear, "You gonna try and win me something?"

He grinned and hollered at the guy. "I might just do that on the way back."

The carny frowned, disgusted he hadn't been able to hook a sucker, then pivoted to call out to other passersby. They moved on, only to be interrupted by two voices calling out from a distance.

"Addi!"

"Oh my gosh, Jax Cooper!"

They swished their gazes around, trying to spot who called out their names. "Up here!"

Chins up. Addi laughed. "On the Ferris wheel! Jenny and Tom. Remember them from high school?" She waved.

It took a slow few seconds, but yes, he did remember. "Hey!" He joined her in waving at the couple, who he couldn't actually see well, since they were nearly at the top of that big wheel now.

They continued their walk toward the food court. A thought struck him. "Weren't those two dating in high school?"

"Jenny and Tom? Yes, they never stopped."

"Hmm. Wow." The old lifeguard towers, the fair, a couple from high school still together ... he was right: In many ways, time stood still in Saltwater Beach.

After ordering food, they found one free table. "We're in luck." Jax grabbed his first corn dog, dipped it in ketchup, and took a large bite.

"Whoa, wait a second." Addi frowned at him. "You did not just put ketchup on your hot dog."

"I did not." He swallowed another bite and grinned. "It's a corn dog."

"Same difference. And everybody knows that corn dogs call for mustard. Every time."

He wrinkled his nose, digging into the second dog. "Not a fan. And anyway, I thought you didn't eat gluten."

"Sometimes I do. I don't have celiac disease—those who do must be very careful about what they eat and how they prepare it." She shrugged. "I just don't really like how gluten makes me feel."

"That's weird."

"You know what's really weird? Ketchup on a corn dog. What happened? Did Chicago do this to you? Have you become the guy who puts ketchup on everything—even eggs?"

He just smiled at her as he ate his dinner.

Addi dropped her corn dog onto its plate and sat back. She was her playful self again. "I'm just not sure we can continue as friends."

He polished off the rest of his food and snapped a look at her plate. "So you're saying that's up for grabs?"

She swiped her food back up and peeled away some of the fried batter from the dog, dropping it onto her paper plate. "I'd forgotten what it was like to hang out with the Cooper brothers so often."

"Meaning?"

"Your mama would call out when dinner was ready, and that's about the only time you boys would willingly go home." She leaned forward. "You might recall I was often invited along."

"My mother liked you."

"Well, the feeling was mutual." She wore a contented smile. "Your mom made enough food for a small army, but still, I had to act fast. You boys were worse than hungry dogs at feeding time."

"Aw, we were precious."

She cracked up. "More like incorrigible."

A man called out "ice cream, ice cream" like they were at Wrigley Field. Without asking for Addi's input, he bought two and put one in front of her. She tore into it like a starved woman.

"Mm. I forgot how good ice cream tasted at the fair."

He nodded and smiled, but his mind had gone elsewhere. He and Addi had been inseparable for many years, even as kids. Why had he let that slip away?

His phone dinged, and Jax forced himself not to grimace at the client's name on the screen. It was Friday night, for crying out loud—and two hours later in Chicago! He stuck the phone in his jacket pocket, thankful that Addi was too focused on her ice cream to notice.

"I just remembered something," she said.

"Yeah? Tell me."

"Ninth inning. Our team was down by two. You're up at bat."

He nodded. "We had two on base."

She froze, eyes wide. "How do you remember that?"

Jax shrugged. "What's to forget? I knocked it out and we walked off the field."

"Sheesh. I can almost hear the *na-na-na-na-na* rolling around in your head."

"You're hilarious."

"Well, obvi, I remembered it too, but what happened after is more vivid in my mind. Do you remember how we all went over to the Dixie Cone to celebrate?"

He thought a moment, dropping his gaze from the sky to her face. Her eyes sparkled as she waited for his answer, and tendrils of her shiny, dark hair lifted on the warm breeze.

Memories? What memories? All he wanted was to lean forward and kiss those ice-cream-coated lips ...

Addi snapped her fingers in front of his mug. "Earth to Jaxson."

He blinked and swiped another bite of his cone. "Sorry."

"You might not remember going over to get ice cream with the team that night, but I do. I'd hardly seen you all season, you were always gone at practice. But Josie begged me to go—you remember her, right?"

"She was trouble."

Addi giggled. "Stop it. She was not."

"Continue."

"Anyway, we showed up, and all the guys were hootin' and hollerin', but you got mad about it."

Jax frowned.

"Don't put that frowny face on—you were upset because all the attention jumped off you and onto us."

A picture of that night hit him like a jolt. The memory clear. Addi was right—he had been ticked when she and Josie strutted into the place with their short skirts and false eyelashes.

But it had nothing to do with losing everyone's attention and everything to do with how the guys started looking at her. She'd changed, seemingly overnight, when in reality, he had been too self-absorbed until then to notice.

Jax swallowed back another bite of cone, but it stuck in his throat. He coughed, trying to shake it loose, but that only made his throat raw. He coughed again, wheezing on the inhale.

"I'll get you some water!" Addi dashed off while he tried to swallow the dry piece of cone.

She returned in a hurry with a small paper cup full of tepid water. He threw it back, and it dislodged the obstruction. He coughed once more to clear his airway.

"You okay?" Addi was bending over him now, her hair tickling his face, her jewel-green eyes showing true concern.

But he didn't deserve her concern. Not now, not then. Clarity had struck him tonight. He remembered now how he had begun to notice the changes in Addi right before their senior year. But instead of building on what they'd developed over the years, he had pushed her away. After all, he would be going away to school soon, so why start something that might ruin their friendship?

The problem was, he didn't want anyone else to have her either. And that's exactly what happened. Other guys noticed her. Lots of them.

"Ready to go?" Addi was standing now, all talk of memories halted.

Fine by him. Jax nodded and stood, then pitched his paper plate into a nearby garbage can.

"If we hurry, I'll have time to beat you at darts again—just like old times."

He chuckled and picked up the pace. "Not a chance."

Twilight fell by the time they made it back to the breezeway filled with carnival games. Sure enough, most families with young children had vanished. A few teens walked in pairs, but mostly, the area had opened up. They could play any game they chose without having to wait.

"There," he said, "that one." He pulled her past several booths, their hosts calling at them, trying to lure them over.

Addi snorted. "You dragged me over to play tub toss."

"I did. Is there an issue?"

"Well, no, but I pegged you as more of a ring toss guy."

He chuckled. "Sure you did."

The carny loaded Jax up with balls. "Get three in the tub and you'll get one of them stuffed dogs."

Addi leaned forward. "Oh! Now I get it." She bumped Jax with her body for the second time tonight, and that same old frustration came over him. He didn't want to be high school pals anymore. "You're trying to win a dog. Ah, Jax. I never knew you to be the sentimental type."

He grinned but kept his eye on the target. "Maybe I'll surprise you." He threw the first ball, landing it right in the bucket.

"Ooh, good one."

Did she remember the last time they were at the fair together? When she had played a game like this and won? He wound up another pitch and—boom! —landed it in the bucket.

The carny nodded. "Nice. Third one gets the prize. Only two gets you the consolation."

He glanced at the barrel full of ninety-nine-cent plastic balls, smirking. He would *not* be walking away from here with one of those. He wound up, then slowed. Why did this seem so familiar? A flicker of something tried to push up through the mess of thoughts in his head. Ugh with the memories already!

Nothing showed itself. He shrugged it off. Probably just the fact that he and Addi had tonight brought back the tradition of attending the summer fair on its first Friday night.

"Ya chicken?" The carny was eyeing him.

He scowled, the memory he had been trying to extract growing clearer. Link had been here the same night, goading him on at every turn. When Addi won a teddy bear that night and gifted it to him, the guy couldn't stop laughing.

"You're whipped, man," he'd said.

Jax hadn't taken that well. What eighteen-year-old kid

would? But then he'd smelled the beer on Link's breath and shrugged it off. The guy had always been a fair-weather friend, the kind that would show up for the free Popsicles after the beach cleanup had already ended.

Jax figured that by the time he left for college, Link Grandfield would be a dim memory. He was right. He had not thought of the guy once in a dozen years, well, not until he had the audacity to appear at his mother's memorial.

The carny broke into his thoughts. "I said, are ya chicken?"

Jax steeled himself then pitched that ball straight into the center of the bucket. Addi squealed and jumped up, cupping his bicep with her fingers. When he handed her the huge white dog as a prize, she leaned toward him before pulling back, like she was about to kiss him on the cheek and then thought better of it.

If she had chosen to kiss him, it would not have been the first time. A picture formed in his head and floated over him like a big cartoon bubble. She had kissed him that night at the fair when they were kids too. The way he recalled it, the night had been perfect. And then it wasn't.

"You're looking pretty serious for someone who just won a prize."

He dropped his gaze to find her peering up at him, pink in her cheeks, and her eyes unwavering on him. He was a grown man with a broken engagement under his belt. So why did stealing a kiss feel akin to criminal behavior?

Maybe because, all those years ago, he thought that a simple kiss would be their start—but it turned out to be their end.

He swallowed back his fear.

"Jax?"

"I want to kiss you."

"You ... want ... to ... kiss me."

A smile tickled his mouth, and his hands found her waist. Despite the noise and chaos surrounding them, her sigh reached his senses. He fought against the tsunami of desire that wanted to crush her to him. Instead, he slowly encircled her body with his arms and breathed her in, a mix of jasmine and sunshine filling him.

"Jax," she whispered.

I know, I know ... the words floated through his mind. He brushed his lips with hers, and when their mouths met, he knew—he had never tasted anything so sweet.

Chapter Seven

Addi stared at the display of meat thermometers hanging near the barbecues that her father had just put on sale for summer. The heat of Jax's touch last night still lingered on her cheeks, and if she shut her eyes, she could revisit the need she had seen in his. She hugged her waist, feeling his arms around her, tugging her against him.

"What're you staring at?"

"Huh? Oh." Addi shook her head. "Sorry, Daddy. Lost in thought."

"Have never known you to be a daydreamer."

"Well, a girl can change."

He grimaced, his chunky glasses on the edge of his nose. "You? Hogwash."

She giggled, the sound of it surprising her. She switched on the old boom box under the counter and moved the dial until a country song came on. Then she cranked it up and began to sway.

"What's wrong with you?"

She raised her brows, pretending not to hear. "Come again?"

Vic marched around to the other side of the counter and pushed the boom box's off button. "What's gotten into you, Addison May? You're acting like a dang teenager!"

"What's wrong with that?"

"What's wrong with—?" His expression was bewildered. "You're too old for that!"

Addi scoffed. She took a long look at her father. The lines in his face had deepened, though she hadn't really noticed how much until right now. "You know what I think?"

He raised an eyebrow. "No, but you're going to tell me anyway, aren't you?"

She shifted. "I think you should go to the fair. I'll stay here and keep an eye on things."

"The fair? Why would I want to go and do a thing like that?"

"Maybe because it's fun." She kept smiling; he wasn't going to stop her. "It's actually old timers' day until two o'clock. I'm sure lots of your friends will be there."

"That supposed to make me happy? You calling me old?"

"You just did that to me! Anyway, seniors get in free."

He weighed that. "I think I'll pass."

"All right, then what about going fishing? When's the last time you took your rod out to the pier for the afternoon? Or, I know, you can take up golf. Start today with a bucket of balls."

Her dad put down the stack of papers he'd been holding onto since the minute he had pulled Addi out of her daydream. "I don't know why all the sudden interest in my life, but for the last time, I'm not interested in having any fun today or any day." He tapped the pages on the counter. "This is my fun! Now, if this is your way of getting out of helping today—"

"It's not."

"Good." He took up the papers again. "I'll be in the office, paying our vendors."

"Suit yourself."

Her father stared after her a hard second before trudging back into that dingy office of his. She sighed and drummed her fingers on the countertop. She hadn't planned to come into the store today, but her father's occasional helper, Sydney, had called in sick.

She pulled in a cleansing breath. Addi suddenly had this abiding urge to bake something, but it would have to wait. Her father often saved his paperwork for Saturdays, which meant he could be in that little room working for hours.

Sigh.

Addi grabbed a bottle of counter spray and a couple of clean rags and began on the north side of the store, wiping down dusty packaging and shelves. With no music to accompany her, she hummed. That's right—hummed. She hadn't felt like humming in, well, she didn't know when.

Last night's fairway blared with country music, giving her plenty of songs to choose from to accompany whatever memory she wanted to. She kept moving and wiping and humming.

Her eyes caught sight of a commotion happening outside the easterly window, facing the town. Cars and pedestrians stopped to let a fire truck speed by, its lights and sirens calling all sorts of attention to themselves.

She frowned. Addi hadn't thought about the fire that consumed much of this place years ago. Her father had rebuilt, though some criticized him for not taking that opportunity to *pretty up* the place. She'd wondered about that, too, but frankly had not contributed much to that conversation.

"You do whatever it is you need to do, Victor," her mom had told him. She wasn't too well then and didn't have a lot of drive in her, but she was always supportive.

She flicked a look out the window where traffic had begun again and strollers crossed at the corner. Addi had seen hundreds of fire trucks speed by over the years but had never revisited their own tragedy. Why now?

She glanced around. Pretty quiet for a Saturday, and she wished that weren't the case. Her mind did not need the fertile ground of silence at the moment. With a quick swipe of a top shelf, Addi finished dusting and tossed the cleaning rags into a bucket beneath the front counter. She would take them home later to wash.

A shadow passed by the front door, and she straightened, ready to serve a customer. The door stayed shut, and she let out a breath. Her racing heart, the one she had started the day with, had slowed. She fiddled with the service bell on the counter, listlessly tapping the chrome top several times in a row.

Her father stuck his head out of the office. "Addi!"

"Yes! Sorry."

He shut the door again. For the past twelve hours she had done nothing but replay last night's visit to the fair with Jax. If she needed to come up with one word to describe it, she would choose *magical*. The stars, the music, the gross food, and oh, that kiss.

But if she were honest, shadows of memories from a long-ago time at the fair had been lurking around the corners of booths and rides. She had been able to ignore them mostly, to lean into all the good that served to erase the bad.

But then that fire engine groaned down Main Street, and now, as she waited here in the quiet, her heart dipped, that old memory of her last time at the fair, when they were kids, rearing its head.

She had awakened early that day, and Chase had found her on the beach collecting sea glass. Already she knew that summer would be bittersweet for her, with Jax and other friends leaving for college as soon as fall rolled around. But she'd had reason to believe that all was not lost.

Friends. During his senior year, Jax had become quieter, less like his old self. Strange for someone whose hopes and dreams were a touch away. By the way he'd acted—ornery, exceptionally quiet, and often just downright glum—she had wondered if they were even still friends.

But that last night at the fair, all Jax's moodiness had disappeared. He had made a college switch just before the deadline, and he was in a celebratory mood. He had been sweet to her all night, jovial, that she'd spent her pennies on a dart game—and won. She had gifted him with a teddy bear, and he'd made a big show of it all night, waving it to onlookers as they passed by, shouting, "She won this for me!"

Maybe it was the headiness in the air or the hint of promise she had for their future after being friends for so long, but when Jax wrapped his arms around her beneath the night fireworks show, she, quite impulsively, pressed a kiss to his smiling mouth.

And he didn't pull away.

She had so many questions after that—would he declare his love for her and beg her to follow him to college? Or ask her to wait for him? But that night, as she lay in bed pondering all these questions, a commotion startled her, a pounding on the front door of their family home that brought her father downstairs in a hurry.

The hardware store was on fire—and to the neighbor who

had seen the flames, it looked bad. Addi had stayed with her mother until morning, and to cheer her up over the loss of her father's business, she had gone to collect sea glass from the beach. Her mother loved the jumble of colors and kept a glass jar full of her finds on her nightstand.

That's when she ran into Chase, his hair mangled, his face dirty from a night of sleeping on sand, exposed to the elements. If she hadn't known him so well, she might have mistaken him for a drifter and run off to safety. But he wanted to talk, and though she needed to get back, she let him rage on.

And that's when he blurted out his secret to her—a catharsis for him, but something altogether different for her.

She exhaled, remembering, the store eerily quiet for a Saturday. Addi never meant to carry a burden this big. Once the words had made their way out of Chase's mouth all those years ago, they could not be taken back ...

She flicked a hard look at him, seawater pooling around her legs, her feet sinking deeper into the mushy, drenched sand.

She crossed her arms. "I don't want to hear another word about this."

"But there's more to tell. Please!"

Addi lifted her hands to her ears, the crush of wind and waves barely stifled. If it kept her from hearing whatever he had left to say, then it would be enough.

Chase pulled one of her hands from her face and held it tightly in his. A deep crease had formed between his eyes, which were both trained, unwavering, on her. She trembled at his desperation. "It's not my fault," he said. "He—"

"Stop it." She pulled away, turning her back on him, and started to jog, knowing she was no match for his stride. If he

wanted to catch up with her, he would. But she had to try. If only running away could erase the secret he had just divulged.

Why had he told her? And why now? So that she had to bear his burden too? It wasn't fair. Didn't she have enough to deal with at home with her mother's illness? Wasn't her future already dim, as compared with his?

Anger ignited her speed until she was running in an all-out sprint down the beach. She gulped air, unaccustomed to using her lungs and limbs like those crazies who did this for fun.

A crush of sadness came over her, and she slowed her pace. Everything was changing—everything except her life. Pretty soon, most would be leaving Saltwater Beach to begin their new lives.

Everyone but her.

Addi turned around now, her fists finding her hips, her breathing a shallow pant. Chase was standing behind her, as she suspected he would be.

"I just want to say that I'm sorry, Addi."

"It's time for you to go."

Addi startled at her father's voice. "What? I mean, no, I'm planning to stay as long as you need me."

"I don't know what's going on in that head of yours, young lady, but I can handle things from here on out." He paused, his eyes not as narrowed, his voice not as grumpy as usual. Her father spoke softly. "Enjoy your Saturday, peaches."

He hadn't called her that in ... wow. It had been so many years since she had heard that pet name she had nearly forgotten about it. Addi took her small cross-body purse from a drawer. She leaned close to her father and kissed him on the cheek. "Thank you, Daddy."

Thirty seconds later, she swung open the door to The

Coffee Hole, ordered a coconut latte and hoped for the best, and headed to the beach, which was a mere three-quarters of a mile down the block. She found a spot on the wall that separated the sand from the sidewalk and took a long swig of her coffee.

Awful. Horrible! She would have to talk to Lily about setting up her coffee cart at the other end of the block. Desperate measures. Addi got up and pitched the nearly full cup into a nearby trashcan.

After slipping out of her shoes, she headed down to the water. Maybe it was time to, finally, bury the old guilt for good. Chase had done that, so why hadn't she?

Cool water from the Pacific Ocean bathed her feet in its softness. She walked along, allowing her thoughts to settle down with each step. Something about being out here with the waves and breeze and nothing much else helped her to think clearly, without all that crowding of regret.

To this day, Addi had wished Chase had not told her what he had done. It wasn't fair of him, and if it weren't for Lily reaching out to her one day when she'd popped into the coffee shop, she might not have ever reconnected with the Cooper family.

"Watch out!"

A Frisbee buzzed by her head. She jerked away, watching it land in the surf. A male jogged over to get it, splashing her in his wake. He plucked the Frisbee from a wave before it was dragged out to sea and flung it fiercely to shore.

"Oh, hey, Addi."

"Nate?" His golden curls were usually dry and covered by a hat. It took a second before she recognized him.

"Yes, ma'am. Day off. Thought I'd get some sun."

"Great day for it."

"Did my sister give you a reprieve today?"

"Lily's handling things today, yes. By the way, she misses you."

A remorseful expression overtook him, his eyes downcast. "Yeah, work's been busy."

"Jax is still in town too."

"Now you're making me feel bad."

"Ha. I doubt that. You're a cop who's seen the worst in people, I suspect. Somehow, I think you're just fine."

"No, really. I do need to stop by the house."

I nodded. "Do it tomorrow evening."

He tilted his head, his gaze questioning.

"Family dinner. I've been invited, so I assume you are too."

"Oh—right. Of course. I'll be there." Someone called out to Nate, and he gestured that he'd be right there. He gave Addi another friendly look. "You'll tell my sister for me?"

But Nate ran off, no doubt already out of earshot as Addi called back, "Sure thing."

Jax slid into the pew next to Lily. He had not been to church in a long, long time, and doing so took him back. Already he had nodded to several familiar faces, and it was likely that, before the morning ended, he would be collared outside by the donut table with questions by some of those faces about his life in Chicago.

Note to self: Avoid the donut table.

He gave the sanctuary a careful scan. Addi had worked all day yesterday, as had he. They would see each other later at the family dinner, but he hoped she would be here this morning as well.

"Why the weird smile on your face?" his sister hissed.

"Good morning to you, dear sister."

She smirked. "Something's up. I can tell by that look on your face."

"And what look are you referring to?"

"Fear and hope all mixed up."

"Then I suppose I'm in the right place."

She laughed loudly, causing an elderly woman wearing a hat style he hadn't seen since reruns of *I Love Lucy* to turn her head and shush her.

Lily leaned forward. "Good morning, Mrs. Krump."

Jax laughed now but quickly covered it with a cough. Lily darted a what's-wrong-with-you look at him. "That's really her name?" he whispered. When she nodded, he added, "Thought you were kidding."

A moment later, Addi touched him on the shoulder. Funny how he knew it was her before he turned to look. He smiled up at her beautiful face and scooted over for her to join him.

But with her hand like a stop sign, she gestured for him to stop. Discreetly, she slid in front of Jax and plopped herself between Lily and him. Lily leaned toward her, said something, and they both laughed together. More words. More laughter.

He hadn't felt like a third wheel in a really long time. And never at church.

Mrs. Krump turned and stared the ladies down, stopping their chatter. Jax snickered and Addi elbowed him hard in the side. He shrank back. "What did I do?" he hissed.

But she only lifted one delicate forefinger to her lips and suggested that he *shh*.

The service began with worship music that, admittedly, he hadn't heard for years. Yet he sang along as if he had last sung those words yesterday. Afterward, Pastor Simon led them in prayer and began his message.

Jax had always prided himself on his focus, and though the pastor's sermon left him with a few nuggets to chew on, he feared that Addi's presence beside him had overshadowed most of it.

An hour later, he tentatively took her hand and led her to the church's courtyard where congregants had gathered. She stopped him with a tug on his fingers.

"I never figured you for a donut man."

"Oh really?"

With a curled index finger, she signaled for him to follow her, which he did down a long hallway and around a corner. He didn't care one whit that she was leading him around like a dog on a leash, and he wasn't about to waste the moment. He pulled her into the space behind a door. "You planning to take advantage of me in the church?" he asked.

"Shh." Addi's green eyes flashed a warning at him. "Lightning can strike indoors you know."

He laughed. "Not true."

"Don't test the Lord."

"Yes, ma'am."

She pulled him into the kitchen and over to a bank of cabinets. She raised up on her toes, pulled a plastic container from a cabinet, and popped the lid, revealing its contents.

Jax inhaled the contents. "Wow."

He attempted to steal a kiss, but she flipped the lid up higher and laughed. "Brownies. They're gluten free."

"You little ... minx."

Addi rolled her eyes. "Hurry up and grab one before I bring them out to the masses."

Outside, people were milling about the coffee and stale

donuts, like old times. Addi slid her box onto the table—minus
one fat square of a brownie—and a type of pandemonium
occurred, with those in-the-know jetting for a gluten-free treat.

Casually, Jax slid his arm around Addi when a familiar face
appeared.

"So it's true!" Jenny Marquez had joined them. "I told
Tom I thought you were a couple, and he said *no way*, but here
you are!"

Addi slid out of Jax's loose grip and gave Jenny a brief hug.
"Hi, Jen. Did you and Tom have fun at the fair? Were your kids
up there with you?"

Jenny sputtered. "The kids? Uh-uh. That was date night
with me and the old man."

"Hey, who's old?" Tom joined them, looking happy if not a
little larger around the middle than he did in high school. Jax
stuck out his hand and Tom shook it. "I was sorry to hear
about your mom."

Jenny cut in. "Oh, yes, Jax. So sorry. She was one of the
nicest ladies. We will all miss her around here."

Jax nodded, though acutely aware of the way both Tom
and Jenny's gazes seem to slide between Addi and him in a
questioning way. To avoid having to answer questions he
hadn't confronted yet himself, he said, "Tell me about you
two."

Jenny looked from her husband and back to Jax again. "Us?
We're just an old married couple now with two kids and a
dog." She laughed.

Tom hooked an arm around Jenny's neck and kissed her
head. "Not true. We're young and gloriously in love, like
always."

Jenny fluttered her eyelashes. "Yes, so true. Especially since
the kids spent the weekend with my parents—woot-woot!"

They all laughed.

"But hey," Tom said, "don't mention we went to the fair without them. They'll hold it over our heads through their teen years. Could be brutal."

Jenny slapped him. "Stop it." She looked up at Jax. "It's so good to see you again—to see you both. You look happy."

Addi stumbled over her words, but ultimately said, "Thank you."

Jax nodded, thanked them, and to keep the conversation off him added, "And you do as well. Have you been in Saltwater Beach since high school?"

Tom nodded. "We have. We took over her parents' exterminator business and run it together. I know what you're thinking—gross."

Jax chuckled. "I wasn't thinking that."

Jenny jumped in. "It was a no-brainer. Coastal areas are simply crawling with termites, which means—"

"Yeah," Tom said, "which means we've been to Hawaii yearly since taking over."

Again, they all laughed. After Tom and Jenny had gone, Jax walked Addi to her car. She leaned into him. "You survived."

He scoffed. "What do you mean?"

She looked up at him now, her face awash in sunlight. He sucked in a breath. His head told him there were things that needed to be sorted, but his heart was having none of it. Her beauty had only been enhanced by the years—years he had missed.

"I mean that you survived the meet-cute with Tom and Jenny, while also successfully avoiding all talk of yourself."

He swallowed. She knew him, didn't she? He had expected to field a barrage of questions about his life away from here, yes. But when he'd turned the questions to them, had he expected to see such joy in their faces? "You're not completely wrong—"

"Ha."

"I didn't know what to expect. It's been a long time since I've been here." He pulled her into a loose hug and looked out into the distance where palm branches bent from the breeze. "I regret not staying in touch with more people."

"Like Jenny and Tom?"

He lowered his gaze to her waiting eyes, knowing exactly who she really meant. He wrapped his arms around her tighter, his voice deep, low. "Who else but two people who could make extermination sound *that* exciting?"

Addi cracked up and thumped him on the chest with her palm. "You're ridiculous."

When she tried to pull away, he cinched her back. Her eyes fluttered under his gaze, and his mouth hovered near her neck. "I missed out on you, Addi," he whispered, and pulled her into his embrace.

* * *

Something Pastor Simon said during the morning's sermon had been turning over in Jax's head. He pulled a Bible out of the drawer in his mother's guest room—she always kept one there—and turned to Proverbs. Olive sat next to him, her chin resting on his knee. Verse nine read: *In their hearts, humans plan their course, but the Lord establishes their steps.*

For as long as he remembered, he had plans to leave his hometown, to get an education, and to live the dream in a high rise in some far-off city. And he had done it. His parents had never tried to convince him to come back home, to live here, even after he'd taken the California bar and passed it. On the contrary, they had been supportive of his dreams, wherever they took him, and he always appreciated that.

But he noticed twinges of disillusionment at times. How often had he taken clients to Cubs games, only to watch them play on their phones the entire time? Or act disinterested in the game? He shook his head. Or what about the Friday nights working past sundown, only to see the bustle and lights of date-night traffic on the streets below?

And though it caused him pain and embarrassment, he had never really faced head-on Mara's reasons for canceling their wedding. *I can't marry someone who won't be honest with me— or with himself.*

He shook his head, remembering her face, her words. Had to. Especially since he had always counted honesty and forth-rightness to be hallmarks in his life and legal career, and she had called him out on something even he had not seen in himself. Something he found himself having to confront the minute he came back to Saltwater last week, when he stepped back into his mother's house.

Addi.

Even though a dozen years had passed, he had never forgotten her. Admittedly, he thought she had married. But looking back, he could not fathom why he would have let that happen without a fight.

He glanced back at the passage that had stuck out to him this morning, wondering what it really meant for the Lord to establish a person's steps. So counterintuitive to what he had studied in law, to how he had lived his own life to this point.

Maybe that was the problem. He had been spinning through life, like on a carnival ride, since the minute he left town. School, study, exams, the bar ... work. Had he ever stopped, even for a minute, to check in with God? Was it he who had set him on this merry-go-round of nonstop activity? Or had he somehow missed a memo?

All he knew for certain was that Addi's presence took center stage now. As well, more questions from long ago had formulated in his mind as of late.

He never knew what happened between his father and Vic, for example. Addi's father had always seemed like a caricature to him, a regular *get off my lawn* type of guy. He never really liked Jax, for whatever reason. But things turned even darker after that fire, which ruined his business.

Jax had always figured it had something to do with his father being a co-owner of the building. Maybe Vic didn't like the amount of insurance coverage, or maybe he was just plain angry that it all happened.

Understandable.

But why take it out on him—a kid? He and Addi had been friends for decades, but he couldn't remember a time when Vic Barrett had ever offered him even a smile.

His mind circled back to his own father. They may not have seen eye to eye on everything, but his father had always been bigger than life to him. A man's man. Someone to look up to and try to emulate.

Maybe one way to do that would be to start by fixing whatever old wound still existed. That's what firstborns were supposed to do—fix things. From all accounts, Lily had stepped in ... and he had been sleeping on the job.

As he stepped into the kitchen with Olive in tow, where Lily was pulling a lasagna out of the oven, he made a mental note to call Vic Barrett in the morning. "What can I help with?"

Lily slid the hot dish onto a couple of trivets. "Dress the salad?" She pointed to a bowl of greens.

He smiled at the assumption that the salad would be dressed as it always had been: olive oil, red wine vinegar, salt and cracked pepper. He dug the ingredients out of the pantry and got to work. There were no dogs in the daycare today, a new provision Lily had implemented for Sundays.

Lily pulled a second lasagna out of the oven. "Whoa. How many are you expecting?"

His sister's eyes flashed. "You think I don't know what I'm doing? Y'all eat like hogs."

Jax sputtered.

"Don't get all insulted." She shut the oven door. "You have no idea what it felt like to be the only girl in a sea of brothers. Mom was always smuggling food to me that she had sneaked away from you guys.

"Oh, please."

"It's true! There were never any snacks around, so she brought care packages to my room."

"Knock, knock." Addi entered the kitchen, and suddenly his brain scrambled. One minute he was pulling her into his arms for a kiss, and the next he felt helplessly inept at knowing what to do around her. At the moment, he was teetering between both scenarios.

Lily interjected while cutting the lasagna into plate-sized squares. "Heard you two were making out at the fair."

"We were not."

Addi's face reddened. "That's not true."

Lily swung around, spatula in the air, and gave a pointed look that said *I ain't buying it*.

"Here," Addi said, taking the spatula from Lily's hand, "let me help you with that."

Lily began to protest when Jax grabbed an open bottle of cabernet sauvignon from the rack. "And here"—he poured a glass and handed it to his sister—"have some wine. We can take it from here."

Lily eyed the wine. She took the glass and slowly backed out of the room but paused, reaching for a basket of bread. "Don't forget to bring the food out after you kiss."

"Lily!"

She laughed and exited the room, wine in hand. Jax reached for Addi.

She waved the spatula over his head. "What're you doing?"

He lowered his voice. "Trying to make this less awkward."

Addi giggled, and he kissed her temple, then let his mouth trail down her cheek until their lips met. His heart told him to milk this moment for as long as possible, but his brain sent out warning signals that beat in his ears.

Olive whined next to them, pawing at Jax's jeans, and the kitchen door swung open. A deep voice broke through. "I'm going to have to see your license and registration."

Addi turned. "Nate?"

"Ma'am. Do you realize this man just ran through a stop sign?"

Jax threw back his head in laughter. Then he grabbed a wadded-up towel from the counter and pitched it at his brother's head.

Addi broke free from Jax's arms. She put on a couple of oven mitts and picked up one of the lasagnas. "Hold the door open?"

Nate winked at Jax. "My pleasure."

Jax rolled his eyes and followed behind Addi, carrying the salad.

At the table, Lucky piped up. "Hope there's no slobber on that food."

"Incorrigible," Jax said.

Addi dashed back into the kitchen for the second lasagna. On the way back in, she said little, but by the pink in her cheeks and the shy smile on her face, he knew she was enjoying the attention. The five of them gathered around, said grace, then promptly dug into the food.

"That gluten free?" Lucky asked Addi as she dished up a square.

"Yes, because your sister is an angel."

"An angel!" Lily smiled. "I've been called a lot of things, but surely never that."

"I'll say." Jax speared a roll. "I want some gluten with my dinner tonight."

Nate took a bite of roll. "We're gonna be all bloaty tomorrow."

Lily frowned. "You did not say bloaty."

He grinned, squishy bread lining his teeth.

Jax sat back. "Wow. Not much has changed around here." Of course, he knew that wasn't completely true, but watching the banter, he felt assured that his mother would be pleased.

Lucky screwed up his face. "Except for, well ..."

"I know. Of course. We all miss Mom," Jax said.

Nate cut in, emotion burgeoning on his face. "Change of subject—I've spoken to Chase."

All conversation stopped at the same time.

Lucky leaned forward. "You have? How?"

"I'm a cop, remember?"

Lucky leaned back, the wind out of him. "Then where is he?"

Nate sat back, too, eyeing them all. "No idea. He said he wanted to take some time to think."

"Of all the thoughtless—"

Addi reached over and put her hand on Lily's, concern etched across her forehead.

Lucky shook his head. "Didn't even bother to call me."

"He didn't call any of us," Jax said.

"But I'm his twin!"

Jax had never seen Lucky so ... angry. This new side of him had showed itself a couple of times this week already.

Addi spoke, her voice gentle. "Nate, did Chase say why he hasn't been home?"

Nate looked directly at Jax. He had seen that expression in a person's eyes before, but only on the witness stand. Nate was trying to figure out how to answer the question.

Finally, he broke eye contact with Jax and turned to Addi. "Yeah."

"Well?" Lily looked thoroughly disgusted, her fingers tapping the table. "He left us here to handle *everything* because *he's* upset?"

Jax tried to soothe the tension in the room. "Maybe he just needs a little time."

"Time?" Lily poured herself more wine, shaking her head. "No. Uh-uh. You don't get to leave me to make all the decisions around here and then not even show up to offer a shoulder to cry on. At least the rest of you offered that." She muttered that last sentence before swigging the wine.

"He's mad at Jax." Nate's commanding voice silenced the room again.

"Him?" Lucky said.

Jax tapped his finger against his chest. "Me?"

Lily's eyes bored into him and she shot forward. "Jax, what did you do?"

Jax shrank back. "I'm as perplexed as the rest of you. Although ..."

"Although what?"

He sent a guarded look Addi's way, then swallowed. Why did he have to bring this up now?

"Spit it out, Jax." Lily looked like she had whenever all her brothers had gotten on her very last nerve. As he recalled, it was often.

"When I called off my wedding—I think you all remember that—he was, how should I say this? A jerk. Said he wasn't surprised." Jax leaned both of his arms on the table now, remembering back. He clasped his hands. "Pretty much declared that it was all my fault."

Everyone in the dining room stared at Jax. Addi looked down at the tablecloth.

Finally, Lily waved a hand through the air. "This makes no sense at all. What would your wedding being called off have to do with Chase not showing up for his own mother's memorial?"

"Well, that's all I got, unless ..." He turned a questioning look on Addi, but when she frowned in response, he added, "Actually, no. That's all I can think of."

Lily stood, her chair making a scraping sound against the floor. "I'm done—I've lost my appetite. But I'll tell you one thing, Jax, as big a jerk as you are, I don't think you have anything to do with Chase's bad attitude and disappearing act."

Jax scrunched his forehead. He narrowed his eyes. "Uh, thank you?"

With Nate offering no more information, the rest of the family finished their food, and one by one, got up to stick their dishes in the sink. Lily had left a sink full of warm, soapy water before she headed up to her room.

JULIE CAROBINI

Addi approached him tentatively. "I think I'll head out now."

He frowned and reached over and threaded his fingers through her belt loops. He tugged her close. "Hey, now, don't be mad at me too."

She shook her head tightly. "Of course not. I just think you need some family time now." Her eyes held a sorrow he couldn't explain.

"Listen," he said, "I've been thinking about your father."

"My father?"

He dipped his chin. "He doesn't like me very much—never did. And I'd like to know why."

Myriad emotions ran through her expression. More than once, he thought she was about to say something, but then she stopped herself.

He leaned his forehead against hers. "I don't expect you to have any answers, you know."

"I know, but my father is very, um, complicated. Don't take it personally."

"Understood. Would you mind if I asked him out for coffee, before I leave?"

"Before ... you ... leave ..."

"I want to talk to him, man to man. I think, perhaps, he had a rift with my father. That may have something to do with how he feels about me."

Addi looked resigned. She took a step back, but he thought he detected a bit of a shrug in her disposition. "Sure, Jax. If you can get him to meet you, I don't have an issue with it."

"Any advice?"

A small smile returned to her face for the first time since Nate made his announcement. "Yeah. Either order it black or with cream. If you order oat milk, you're done."

Jax nodded, offering her a grin. "Noted." The phone in his pocket buzzed, and he fished it out. He snapped a look at Addi. "I need to take this."

Addi broke free of him, and he felt the loss. "Sure. Right. Of course."

"Call you tomorrow?" he asked over his shoulder.

"Mm-hm."

He turned and kissed her on the cheek then dashed upstairs, answering the call as he took them two at a time.

Chapter Eight

Addi stepped into her apartment, tossed her keys and purse onto a chair, and slipped off her shoes. She padded across the tiny living room and flipped on the fake fireplace, watching as the orange, yellow, and blue flames danced in front of her.

Oh, how she wished for actual heat. Though the early summer days were warm, nights grew cold on the coast, especially this far north. She pulled a knit blanket from a basket and wrapped it around her, straining to hear distant waves.

It was no use. She couldn't get comfortable. She threw off the blanket and marched over to the kitchen, opening the pantry door wide, scanning the baking shelf for ingredients. Walnuts, almond flour, raisins ... bingo. She hauled everything out, plus all the Thanksgiving spices she could find, then foraged through the fridge for carrots, eggs, and cream cheese.

Addi admired her stash. "You are going to become one marvelous batch of carrot cake, my friends."

For the next few hours, she beat eggs, blended ingredients into batter, baked, and taste tested. As she did, the tension that had crept in during the Cooper family's Sunday dinner had lessened some. She hadn't quite digested how those dark clouds rolled in so quickly during an otherwise lighthearted evening.

Poor Lily. Did her brothers have any idea how much she put into those dinners? Into her mother's life those last few years? Into trying to keep the family together despite each member's idiosyncrasies?

She sighed. Of course, these were observations from afar. While she had been made to feel part of the family, Addi was still an outsider. An outsider who had no idea what it was like to truly live in the midst of sibling chaos.

Addi mixed up homemade cream cheese frosting and, after everything had cooled, applied layers and layers of the sugary goodness. Jax had mentioned that he hoped to find Chase "before I leave Saltwater," and she was trying not to obsess over his leaving.

It was nearly midnight before she allowed herself to sit on a stool and admire her work. She swiped her finger through the cream cheese frosting, sneaked a lick, and sighed. Fluffy, moist, dusted with chopped nuts ... how was she ever going to consume all of it? More importantly, she loved it so much—why didn't she bake more often?

Her father never seemed all that interested in what she made, but her mother dearly loved baking. Addi took another swipe of frosting and ate it, reviewing it as she nibbled it down. Could use a little less sugar, but it was perfectly smooth and had the right amount of vanilla. A win, for sure.

She might not have had the chaotic life that a family of seven would endure, but Addi cherished all the time she spent with her mother. She wouldn't change those years, and more often, found herself needing to do the things that bound her and her mother together.

I thought you didn't eat gluten. She smiled, thinking back to Jax's surprise that she would dare to eat a corn dog. True, she *had* been kind of bloated ever since Friday night, but the truth was her mother had celiac disease. So Addi learned to bake for *her*.

Her phone buzzed. A text from Lily: *Sorry I left without saying a proper goodnight. Forgive me?*

She grimaced, not because of what Lily said, but because a part of her wished Jax had sent the text. He had run upstairs tonight quickly, giving her yet another glimpse into what his daily life looked like. Addi shook her head slightly. A month ago, she had no idea that today she would be entertaining a future she had long given up on.

And yet, was Jax entertaining it too? What would a relationship, a real one—not this short-term one—look like? And ... was she getting ahead of herself?

Addi ran her thumb over the message from Lily, realizing that she had missed an earlier text from Pastor Simon. Oh. When did text messaging become as overwhelming as email? She overlooked her email messages more than she cared to think about, causing pathetic responses overloaded with emojis to apologies for the delay.

Hello, Addi. When would be a good time for us to sit down and talk? I will ask Annette to place it on the calendar.

She made a mental note to text Pastor Simon back in the morning. She had a hunch he was going to express his concern over her father's ... health. Addi blew out a breath. See, now this is why she enjoyed baking rather than phone scrolling.

Baking for her was like dawn patrol for surfers—something she had to do often or go crazy.

Which begged the question: Why wasn't she completely insane by now? She really should text Lily back, too, but thought better of it. Addi wouldn't want to wake her. She was about to drag herself off to bed when her cell phone rang, a rarity so late at night.

Jax?

"I'm glad I caught you up. I didn't wake you, did I?"

His voice both soothed her and put her on alert. Was that a good thing or no? "Not at all. I was ... well, I was just about to get ready for bed."

Quiet on the line.

"Are you there, Jax?"

"Mm-hm. Yes. I was, uh, picturing that."

She let out a tiny gasp, followed by a laugh.

"Sorry."

"No apology necessary."

Jax's voice sounded tentative. "I'm sorry I had to take that call."

"It's okay. The night was pretty much over by then anyway."

"Hm, yes. I'd like to apologize for all that too, and I plan to make it up to you." He paused, concern edging his tone. "It's not necessary to drag you into our family's issues, Addi."

"You have nothing to apologize for. Naturally, emotions were high tonight after Nate's, uh, announcement."

"About that—I have no idea what Chase meant and why he has a problem with me."

"Have you ever asked him?"

"No, because whatever it is, it's nonsense."

Silence.

"You think that's harsh of me to say?"

"I think ... I think if it were my sibling, I would want to know if I had done something to offend him or her."

He was quiet a moment, as if chewing on her words. Or maybe she had completely insulted him.

He exhaled, the sound of it like a groan. "You think I'm the jerk."

"No one's calling anyone a jerk. I ... I just hate for all this bad blood to be between your siblings and thought maybe you could get to the root of it."

"You mean work a little harder."

She flinched. "I didn't say that."

"So I could yank it out like a bad tooth, I mean. "

"Well, yes..." Addi was becoming used to Jax's voice and how he sounded when he was working through something. "That's one way to put it."

Silence.

"Addi?"

"Yes."

"Thank you for being honest with me. I know this problem, whatever it is, won't likely go away after one conversation, but you have given me something to think about."

They hung up after Jax promised to check in with her tomorrow evening. Addi replayed their brief conversation in her mind, but couldn't shake that Chase's absence was more than simple sibling rivalry. She leaned her head against the couch pillows, letting her eyes loll to the sound of distant waves.

It's not my fault! He—

She bolted up from the couch. Addi pressed her fingers to her forehead and began to pace, her mind swaying between dreamland and reality. An old ribbon of a memory played through her head now, one that, unfortunately, wasn't a dream at all.

More like a nightmare.

Chase had found her on the beach. Told her things, but after making his admission to her, he swore her to secrecy afterward and had never mentioned it to her again. Not in twelve years!

Could Chase still be angry at Jax after all this time? How was it possible to hold a grudge so long? She blinked, letting her gaze ping-pong around the dimly lit room.

Then again, Jax rarely came back to Saltwater. Would Chase's venom have been on display if he had? Because Jax said his relationship with Chase had changed, and he was in the dark about why.

Addi pressed her palm into her cheek and lowered herself back down to the couch, curling herself into a ball. Was it possible she held the key to all of this? But if she told Jax the truth, her father would find out too. She cradled her face in her hands, wishing it all away. Her father would never forgive her for not speaking up before now.

Lord, what do I do about all of this? You know so much better than I what the best plan of action is. All I feel like doing right now is running away ... like Chase.

Plan of action. Pastor Simon had spoken on Sunday about a person's plans and how the Lord needed to be the one to determine the steps. She had looked up the passage in the book of Proverbs, but it was an earlier passage that stuck out to her even more: *Commit to the Lord whatever you do, and he will establish your plans.*

Had she committed all this to the Lord? Or was she just frittering away her time, hiding from the truth?

The truth will find you out.

Addi sat up again. Chase had posted about truth on his Facebook account, and then went deeper into hiding. She exhaled, allowing that reality to filter through her. In a moment, she knew what she'd feared had come to fruition.

Chase was holding a grudge so deep it had twelve-year-old roots.

The last time Jax felt this nervous he was walking into Judge Monroe's courtroom for the very first time. Known for his ice-cold courtroom and searingly tough demeanor, Monroe wasn't to be trifled with. Except for a slight stutter and sweat rolling down his temples, Jax had come through unscathed. Fast forward three years, and Judge Monroe had even complimented him the next time Jax appeared before him.

Could he dare to hope this coffee meetup with Vic Barrett might produce similar results?

He glanced around from his seat, taking in the *ambience*, as Addi might call it. Plain. Disheveled. Dark. This little shop on the corner of Main Street had potential, if only someone with a vision would take it over.

Why do you care? You won't be around to see it.

He twisted his lips, his thoughts mocking him. Not the first time this week Jax had pondered things that surprised him. He stopped by the police station yesterday, scouring for any information he could about Chase's whereabouts. Just having to do something like that shook him up.

He took a sip of what the menu called a latte, though it was a poor representation. Unfathomable in these times, especially with the beach crowd close enough to walk over. If they weren't careful, the chain store near the highway might move in.

The thought pained him.

He shifted, his mind on overdrive. Lily and Addi should take this place over. Lily could even use her proceeds from selling the house. The women already worked well together. With Lily's top sergeant organization and management skills and Addi's love of baking, this coffee house would rarely have an empty seat.

But then Addi would be here ... while he was in Chicago. He swallowed another swig of coffee and glanced out the window, as if cleaning the palette of his mind. That's when he caught sight of the hardware store owner stepping inside the shop.

Vic approached him, a wary, almost-tired expression in his eyes. Jax stood. He reached out to shake the man's hand. "I'd like to buy you a cup of coffee, sir. What can I get you?

"Why're we here?"

"As I mentioned, I would like to talk to you about some personal matters, sir."

Vic eyed him. Finally, he said, "Plain, black, large."

"You got it." Jax left and returned a moment later, handing the older man his coffee.

Vic took a gulp, no warmer to Jax than when he had first walked in.

Jax cleared his throat. Why was having a conversation with this man more difficult than deposing a disgruntled opposing party? "I've been enjoying spending time with your daughter. She is a beautiful person."

The man was quiet. "Yes. She's a good girl. But I don't want to talk about you and my daughter."

"Neither do I."

"Oh?"

"I care for Addi, but that's not why I asked you here."

"Then why did you?"

Jax gathered his thoughts. "You know that my mother has passed on recently."

Vic nodded, a pain easing across his face. "Condolences."

"Thank you." Jax folded his hands on the table. "I've been away from Saltwater for some time, and it's good to be back."

"For your mother's funeral?"

"To see my family. And reacquaint myself with—"

"My daughter. You said you didn't want to talk about her."

Jax narrowed his eyes on old Vic. "I sense you don't like me very much."

Vic scoffed, looked away, then eyed Jax. "You think real highly of yourself, don't you?"

"But apparently you do not."

The old man leaned forward on the table, his elbow bent, and protected his cup of coffee with his spare hand.

Jax continued. "I would like you to clear up whatever happened between you and my father."

"Your father?" Vic's voice rose, eliciting several turned heads from nearby tables. "The man's dead. Why would you go and bring him up?"

The truth stung even now. If he wanted to, Jax could reach forward and wrap his hand around the man's throat and ... He exhaled a long sigh. Somehow, an act of violence might not go over very well in this small town. Even though he felt sure some would approve.

"My father was a good man. A great father. He took especially good care of you after your business burned."

Vic narrowed his eyes until Jax wondered if he could still see out of them. He pushed his chunky glasses up his nose and spoke through gritted teeth. "Your father burned down my business."

Jax's hands, though wrapped around a hot cup of coffee, went cold. "Why would you say that?"

"Because it's true. He did it for the insurance money."

Jax's hand tightened into a fist. "That is a lie."

"It's why he sold this place soon after. The man was embarrassed that he'd been caught."

Jax stood, toppling his paper cup of crappy coffee, not caring who heard him. He focused on Vic. "My father sold this building during a bad market. He didn't come out ahead—and he certainly didn't do something as heinous as you are implying."

"Oh, yeah? How do you know?"

Jax bent, his face even with Vic's. "Because I knew my father."

"In other words, you don't know." Vic took a drink of coffee and stood taller now, as if anger and caffeine gave him a false sense of power. He lifted his chin.

"You have no proof of what you're claiming," Jax said. "It's absurd."

"Don't need any. Your father didn't win in the end. He begged me not to file a claim with his insurer. Said he wanted to handle it. But I knew what he was up to."

Jax searched Vic's face for some telltale sign of having made up every word of his accusation. When he couldn't find one, he hunted through his brain for a remnant of a memory of the night of that fire.

All he could remember was he'd been to the fair then out to the beach with some friends around the time the fire happened. The next few weeks were a blur to him as he prepared to move away. His parents were occupied by their business dealings. And then, right before he left, Addi announced she was engaged.

Even now, the memory of her announcement haunted him. Had he known she and what's-his-name were even together?

Jax wished he could shut his eyes and shake away that memory. Instead, he kept them trained on Vic Barrett, who stared back at him as if he thought he had won this round.

He had not.

Though Jax could not remember every detail of that time period from the past, he knew one thing: He had heard nothing at all about what Vic claimed. Not a thing.

He crushed his cup and tossed it into the waste can on his way out. It was all a lie. Every bit. And he was going to prove it.

Chapter Nine

Addi awoke on her living room couch, a blanket over her, the pretend fire still burning. Slowly, she stretched then dropped the blanket to the floor and got to her feet. Minutes later, she emerged from the bathroom, her mind still not yet awake. That's when she spotted the carrot cake sitting on her kitchen counter, a large square missing.

Right. She remembered now. Addi had fed her angst last night, right after she realized that Chase's disappearance likely had something to do with his twelve-year old secret. The one she had buried too.

With a shake of her head, she reached for a glass and filled it with cool water, then drank it down. When it didn't revive her enough, she made a pot of coffee. The earthy aroma ballooned around her, and as her eyes began to focus, she looked at the clock on her stove.

Ten-thirty?

Addi bunched her forehead into a frown. That couldn't be right. The clock must need a battery or something. No way would she sleep that late.

She poured the hot coffee into a mug and took an exaggerated sip, not even bothering with cream. Life began seeping its way through her body more fully now. She thought again about the time and hurried into the living room, digging through her bag. She checked her phone.

Ten-thirty-one! Addi peered out the window, her eyes aching against the onslaught of light. What in the world ...

Her father and Jax would already have had their morning coffee meet up. She glanced at her phone again. Neither one had called or texted. She sipped the coffee while staring out the window and tried to picture the two of them sitting across from each other, talking about who-knew-what. No call? No text? Should she be suspicious?

An hour later, after hearing nothing, Addi arrived at the Cooper house. She had put on a sundress and sandals, the easiness of her outfit not quite fitting her mood. Instead of going around back, as she would usually do when working in the doggy daycare, she stood on the front porch and debated about knocking.

"What are you doing, lurking about?" Lily called out from the side of the house where Melanie's garden rambled along. She wore an oversized hat and held rusty clippers.

"Those look dangerous," Addi said.

Lily snorted. "Found them half-buried in the dirt out there, and thought I'd see if I had a green thumb or not."

"And the verdict is?"

Lily wrinkled her nose. "So far, it's a big negative. But, hey, I'm trying."

"That's all we can do sometimes." Lily continued to look at Addi, a question in her eyes. "Fine. I'm here looking for your brother."

Lily gave her a resigned half-smile. "I kinda figured." She

came around the side of the house, took the steps to the porch, and lowered her voice. "He's on a rampage right now, tearing through Mom's office. Not sure what he's looking for."

Addi poked a hand into her waist. "Well, Lily, did you ask him?"

"I decided I needed fresh air and came out here instead."

Addi looked her up and down. "Hence, the overalls."

Lily chuckled. "I never claimed to have fashion sense." After a pause, she exhaled and shook her head slowly. "As far as my brother, he basically told me he would know it when he saw it. In other words, mind my own business."

Addi bit her lip. She turned toward the road, but Lily stopped her. "I didn't say all that to frighten you. Go on." She turned Addi back around with a laugh. "Go get him out of the office, if you can. I think he needs his own dose of fresh air or something."

Inside the house, she encountered Olive curled up by the closed door at the end of the hall at the top of the stairs. Though Addi had never been inside, she remembered that Melanie spent time in there on both hobbies and bookwork. Her heart squeezed. It wasn't an easy job he had right now, going through his mother's papers.

Olive ran her nose up Addi's pant leg. "Aw, so sweet. Have you been out here long?" She gave the good girl several pets.

Olive conveyed her yes by pushing her noggin into Addi's hand while peering upward with her one eye.

Addi breathed in deeply. She leaned close to the door. "Knock, knock. Jax?"

The door opened. Jax peered out, the hollows beneath his eyes deep. "Hi."

"You okay?"

"Been better." He kissed her on the cheek, but his eyes sagged, his crow's feet elongated.

She frowned. "You sounded good last night ... when I talked to you on the phone."

He ran his hand through his hair twice. Was it the caffeine he'd consumed with her father that was causing him to be so fidgety? He flashed heavy-lidded eyes at her. "Sorry. I'm looking for something and it's"—he blew out a sigh, and pressed his lips together briefly—"frustrating, to say the least."

"Oh, Jax."

"Finding plenty of other things, but not what I was looking for."

"I'm sorry to hear that."

He stared at her. She stared back. Jax pushed away from the doorjamb. "Where are my manners? Come in."

Addi followed him into the room, and she immediately felt the impact of walking on what she could only describe as sacred ground. This was Melanie's sacred space. She spent hours up here in this office-slash-sitting room.

Breezy floral curtains billowed around the tall, wood-framed windows. A wooden desk with drawers on one side sat beneath one of the two windows. A white-painted file cabinet stood next to the desk, topped with a jumble of family photos.

The entire room was light and feminine, just like her.

She gestured to an old cane rocker in a corner. A tall lamp and a basket of books were nearby, and Addi imagined Melanie relaxing here after a long day. "May I sit?"

"Please." He stacked the papers he had been sifting through onto the desk.

Olive's gaze slid from Addi to Jax and back again. Clearly, the animal sensed some sort of disruption and was trying to decide who needed her comfort more.

"What are you looking for, Jax? Is it anything I could help you find?"

His eyes clouded. He folded his tall frame into his mother's small desk chair and leaned his head in his hands.

When he didn't answer, she added, "You're worrying me. What's wrong?"

He looked up. "What do you know about the night your father's hardware store burned down?"

"I ..." Uncomfortable heat wound its way through her body. One window was open already, but she fought the urge to get up and fling open the other one.

"What I'm asking is, did your father make any claims against mine that you know of? Can you think of anything?"

"I'm not sure what you mean." Addi turned her hands over, gesturing to him how little she remembered about that night, about her father's reaction. "That was a terrible night, to be sure. But I stayed with my mother so he could sort it out. As far as I know, your dad, being the landlord and all, worked everything out for my father to rebuild the store."

"And that's all you know?"

That suffocating heat traversed through her body again. Her heart started beating faster, but not in the way Jax's presence might otherwise cause. More in a *am-I-about-to-have-a-heart-issue?* way. She clasped her hands in her lap and held on tight. "A sad, sad night but ... Mom needed me by her."

His mouth settled into a grim line. He nodded. "Understood. Like you, I don't remember a whole lot about that time. And I can't say that I ever spoke to my parents about it. It's ludicrous, when you think about it. They owned the building back then." He shook his head. "I must have been pretty locked away in my own dreams to not have at least spoken to them about all that transpired."

"You were getting on with your life away from here. As for me, I remember spending time with my mother, distracting her from all of that."

"It must have been quite upsetting for her."

Addi nodded, her gaze drifting toward the open window. Her mother was the mistress of avoidance. She could put on a big smile, wrap herself in a robe, and putter around the kitchen where all worries could be put off for thirty minutes at 350 degrees. Addi could not begin to count the number of times she and her mother had baked instead of giving into worry. Those times had become their love language.

"The thing is, I can't find any record of an insurance claim, but I do see that my father wrote a check to yours for a large sum."

"That was probably the insurance money, don't you think?"

"Hm. Maybe." He hung his head for a moment. When he looked back up at her, pain threaded his gaze. "Your father tells a different story."

She shifted, her hand finding Olive's soft head. "Oh, really?"

Their eyes met. "He says my father paid him off ... that he started the fire himself somehow."

Addi's hand stilled.

He continued. "But I know that could never be true. My father had his faults, but starting a fire for insurance money?" He shook his head. "I know in my gut that's not true."

Addi rifled through her mind, trying to recall what she had heard from her father about that night. He was angry. Discouraged. But also, tight lipped. Anger filled her. How could he level such an accusation? And after so much time, when Mike and Melanie were not here to defend themselves?

Disappointment filled her too. She didn't know all that happened—why her father would think such a thing had occurred—but she also knew, without a doubt, that Mike Cooper had nothing to do with starting that fire.

Still, was it her story to tell? She had promised she never would. But would that promise matter now, after so many years had passed?

Her insides began to quake at the accusation about Jax's dad coming from her father, no less. He had never said anything like that to her! Then again, he never did like Jax ... or Chase ... or any of the Cooper family all that well. She suspected envy had something to do with that.

Sorrow wended its way through her insides now. If only her mother were here to talk this out. Surely, there was some sort of explanation. Or maybe ...

Maybe her father was everything he seemed: an angry man. Life sure didn't play out the way he planned, so he had spent the last thirty years taking it out on others. And frankly, himself.

The sorrow in Jax's face became unbearable. Chase should be here. He could clear this up in an instant. But for whatever reason, he had taken himself out of the picture.

And so, it fell to her.

"Chase ..."

Jax looked up sharply. "Is there something you want to tell me about Chase?"

She ran her tongue over her upper lip, pulling her courage together.

But Jax didn't give her a chance. He pointed a stony gaze at her, one she imagined he pulled out during tough depositions. It seemed to have come out of nowhere. "Were you dating my brother?"

Addi snapped her chin back. "Excuse me?"

"You've been awfully worried about him." Jax ran his hand across his neck, but he kept his eyes on her. "Tell me the truth —have you two been seeing each other?"

"No." She hated the hiss in her own voice, the hurt that came through. But maybe the question wasn't so out of the ordinary. If the tables were turned, wouldn't she wonder the same thing?

Jax stared at her, his eyes reflecting hurt and anger.

She found her courage. "Chase caused the fire at my father's store."

Jax's gaze zeroed in on her. His brows dipped, disbelief woven through his eyes.

"I'm sorry to have to be the one to say it, but it's true."

"It's not."

She reached out and touched his arm, but he flinched. "He"—she stopped and whispered, "This is so hard."

Jax's expression turned even more steely. His jaw clenching. "What is?"

"He told me, Jax. Chase told me that he was the one who started the fire that burned my father's store."

"When?"

She tilted her chin.

His tone turned insistent. "When did he tell you this? When did he confess?"

"The day after it happened when we ran into each other on the beach."

"But ... why? Help me understand this. Why did he tell you?"

"I wish I knew. I've played this over in my head a thousand times, Jax. Honestly, I think it was an unlucky coincidence for me that we were on the beach at the same time." She pushed out a sigh and sat back, allowing her gaze to travel outside the window toward the west. "He needed someone, and I happened to be there."

Silence crackled between them for one long moment.

He was peering at her now, his chin low. "Why didn't you ever say anything?"

"He swore me to secrecy."

"But ... but this was your father's livelihood! How could you keep something like that such a ... a secret?"

She balled a fist. His accusatory tone might work in a deposition or court of law, and it surely would have crippled her as a teen, but now, after all life had served up to her, she didn't appreciate him talking to her that way. Not at all.

She snapped a hard look at him. "There's more. And you need to hear this. Chase was angry at ... you."

"Me?" Jax's own balled up fists opened wide. "Whatever for?"

Addi looked away. She did not come here for a fight, but at this moment, she began to question herself.

"Remind me," Jax said, "when did the fire happen?"

She lifted her eyes to his. "It was the night you made your college decision, well, your second decision. The final one. Do you remember?"

"No."

"You changed schools in time to change your mind and were really happy about it. We all went to the fair that night ..."

His eyes bored into hers. She took a breath and continued. "And after I left, you and your friends headed off to the beach."

He was quiet for several long seconds. "You've held this inside for so long, Addi. I've asked myself for years why you retreated that summer. I— I assumed it had to do with ... Bradford." He spoke her ex's name like it was a four-letter word. "I really hated that guy."

"I know."

"Was that not the case?"

"No." She shook her head. "It wasn't."

"Then why?" He was pleading with her now, his gaze frighteningly still.

"Because"—she swallowed back the memory—"because I was protecting you."

"Addi, why? What did I have to do with any of this?"

A ball of emotion caught in her throat. Her voice cracked. "You were the one who got Chase drunk that night."

Jax narrowed his eyes, disbelief in them. His body language told her he thought she was making it all up.

She stood, sweat making an unwelcome appearance on her skin.

But his eyes widened, as if dawning had come. He reached out to stop her. "I was partying ... excited that I'd been able to get into my dream school."

"Right."

"A bunch of us went to the beach with beer." He hooked eyes with her. "Chase was there."

"Sixteen-year-old Chase."

"Oh no."

She let out the breath she had been holding, a small amount of relief flowing through her that this long-held secret finally was out in the open. "Apparently he got really drunk and did something very stupid involving a cigarette behind my father's store."

Jax expression changed, though, as he absorbed this news. He trained an unyielding gaze on her. "I still don't understand why you kept this a secret all this time."

"You don't?"

Jax stood and began to pace. He stopped in front of her. "Do you realize that my brother has been wearing this guilt for twelve years? And now he's missing?"

Heat rose in her chest and spread down her arms. She curled her hands into fists. "Tell me you're not blaming Chase's decision on ... me."

Jax scrubbed his hand over his scalp. She was beginning to notice how often he did that when he was troubled. "At the very least," he said, "you could have mentioned this news at my mother's memorial. It might have given us some insight into how serious his disappearance could be."

"Jax, are you kidding me right now?"

"Keeping this from us all these years did more harm."

"No. Getting your little brother drunk and leaving him to fend for himself—that's what caused all this harm."

"You should have told Chase to confess, rather than let it fester."

Addi stood. Something she had worried about for the past dozen years was coming to fruition: She was being blamed, when her motivation had always been to protect his future.

Well, she was done. She refused to listen to this nonsense for one more second. Addi stalked across the room and reached for the door handle but spun back around with one more missile to aim at him. "None of this is my fault, Jaxson. If you were thinking with your right mind, you would know that. Chase asked me not to say anything, and I agreed. Not for him, but for you."

He scoffed. "Me?"

"I hated that you were leaving me behind to go off to school. Hated it! And I knew you'd never come back. But ... I cared for you and didn't want to see your dreams derailed by a stupid mistake. I kept the truth quiet—even from my father—for you."

She didn't know what she expected, but Jax's stony gaze wasn't in the running. Did she think he would suddenly pull her into his arms and shower her with his gratefulness? Declare his love for her?

Instead, his jaw hardened. Anger seeped from him. But for once in her life, Addi did not feel compelled to take responsibility for that. Those days of taking on everyone else's problems were over.

She opened the door and tossed a "see you around" over her shoulder.

"Addi?"

She hesitated but turned around anyway, trying to tamp down the remnant of hopefulness rising inside of her. His expression hadn't changed.

"I'll be leaving soon. I've been offered the partnership and have decided to take it."

Addi dropped her gaze to Olive. The pup gave Jax a lingering look then slowly sidled over to Addi, who pressed her lips together and acknowledged his decision with a nod. Then she let Olive out and shut the door behind them, a little more forcefully than necessary.

Addi entered the hardware store at twilight, angrier than she had ever been. Her mind hadn't quite caught up to the whirlwind of thoughts that brought her here, the ones prepared for battle. She stood at the entry, catching her breath, vaguely aware of the scent of skunk wafting through the place, which was, by the way, quite empty of customers.

She fumed.

As she'd torn out of the Cooper house, Olive at her heels, Lily called after her. "Aren't you staying for dinner?"

She had spun around, tears pressing against her eyes. "Go on, Olive. Go to Lily." The poor animal looked so forlorn, like she wanted to make everything all better, but didn't have a clue where to start or what to do.

Oh, could Addi ever relate to that.

Addi had not stuck around long enough to answer Lily's questions or address the fully confused expression on her face. She couldn't, not when all she could think about was confronting the man who had caused the drama that had sent Jax into a spiral this morning. And had done the same to her all her life.

She found her father in the back of the dimly lit store, putzing around with some old model cars he kept back there.

"It stinks in here," she said.

He turned around, his lips pursed. "Well, hello to you too, young lady."

"You need help, Dad."

His lighthearted expression darkened some. "If you have something to say, spit it out."

She crossed her arms. "Were you high this morning when you met Jax for coffee?"

He frowned, his glasses missing. "I don't know what you're talking about."

She exhaled, working to calm herself. "Why did you tell Jax his father burned down this place for the insurance money? What a thing to say."

"He tell you that?"

"Don't deny it."

Her father continued to shine up some of the barbecue

skewers that sold all summer long. He held one up to the light and scrutinized it, squinting. "I never liked that kid. Not then, not now."

"That makes no sense, Daddy. The Coopers are good people."

He turned to her, his eyeglasses sliding down his nose, his gaze hovering over the top of them. "Good people don't try to ruin someone else's life's work just to profit from insurance money. I don't like talking ill of the dead, but you need to face the truth."

"No, you need to face the truth."

His forehead bunched. "Which is?"

She plunked her purse on the counter and held up her fore-finger. "Number one, you are an addict who needs help. Ever wonder why this place is practically empty all the time?" She flung her arm open wide. "Nobody wants to come in here because they would have to deal with you."

Her father's expression changed in a way she had never seen. The corners of his mouth drooped. She had hurt him and knew it, but it did not stop her from her tirade.

She held up a second finger. "And number two, Mike Cooper did not burn down your business."

"And you have a crystal ball, do you?"

"Chase caused the fire—and it was an accident, Daddy. An accident."

"Impossible."

"He dropped a cigarette into a bucket behind the shop, totally thinking it was out. But it spread to the dry fence out back and then over to the back wall." Both freedom and terror wound its way through her. Finally, she could let the truth be known, but at what cost to Chase? Would he ever return home to his family?

Her dad dropped a fist onto the counter. He shook his head and looked squarely at her. "If that was true, I would have heard about it. Stop making up stories. You are not a kid anymore, Addison."

She stepped up closer to him, pointing a finger in his face while trying not to breathe in the stench coming off of him. "You never heard about it because Chase confessed to me and I never told anyone. Not even Jax. Not until now!"

His eyes narrowed so tightly they nearly disappeared. His face, already flushed from his addictions, reddened more. She took no satisfaction in seeing her father angry, flustered, and in fact, her hands shook at what felt an awful lot like disrespect.

But Addi had grown tired of all her father had done to alienate the people she loved.

"You kept this from me?" he accused.

Don't back down, don't back down.

"You chose the Cooper family over your own father?" He hissed at her now. "Why would my daughter, my flesh and blood, do such a thing?"

"Stop making this all about you when it is not. The fire was a terrible, terrible thing, but you survived. We all did." She paused, collecting herself. She would not cry ... she would not! "Mom and I grew closer during that time, when you were so busy rebuilding things."

His expression softened briefly before hardening up again.

She continued, flashing a direct look at him. "I want to know something ... why did you hate Jax so much when we were kids? Before the fire."

Her father exhaled. "Addi ..."

"Because he was my friend. My best friend." She sniffled. "But I could never invite him over."

"He was no good for you."

"I told you we were friends!"

"I could see it in his eyes that he had other ideas."

"Meaning ...?"

"Addison, the man wanted to take you away from here. There. I said it." A weariness overtook him now, and he found his way to a stool near the back counter. A twinge of pity replaced the righteous anger Addi had marched in here with. "I was already losing your mother. I could not lose you too."

A bigger picture of what was happening behind the scenes in her father's heart and mind appeared before her. Finally, she was gaining a small understanding, but she wished she'd had an inkling back then of what was driving him. How different might her life have turned out if she'd had the where-withal to talk to her father plainly during those pivotal years when moving from tomboyish teen to starry-eyed young adult?

Addi took a deep breath, trying to clear her head of all the anger she had been carrying not for days but years. She coughed, the aftermath of pot smoke filling her lungs. Oh, how she hated that smell! Her eyes ringed with irritation. Or maybe unshed tears were causing the redness and pain.

She snagged her father with a look. "That is the most selfish thing I have ever heard. You did everything in your power to keep me tethered to home—when you should have been encouraging me to follow my heart, my own dreams."

"I did what I had to do. You have a good life here, Addison. A very good one. Your own apartment ... two jobs that you love. One day you will inherit all this too."

Addi let her gaze travel around the store and back to her father, who continued to shine up barbecue tools even as they had the most serious conversation of her life. "Good, yes. But if I were to be honest, this is not the one I wanted."

His expression faltered, but her father did not stop from shining those tools.

Slowly, Addi turned around and walked out of the hardware store, a whisper on her heart. *And now it's too late.*

* * *

Being in the wrong was not the normal day-to-day for Jax. Quite the opposite. It's why his bosses at the law firm called him the Wonderkid. It also explains why he was just offered a very generous benefits package and the title of junior law partner.

In the last three years, after his initial training at a smaller, less impressive law firm, Jax had won every case that he had taken to trial. Every. Single. One.

He had made an art—and a large paycheck—from being very, very right.

A wave of saltwater rolled up the sand, dallied on the shore, then retreated into the sea. Jax hooked an arm around Olive's neck, drawing her close to his side as they watched the tide. Lily had mentioned something about giving the pup a bath today for something special, but they had been watching the waves since dawn broke, a byproduct of his inability to overcome his thoughts and get back to sleep. The only times in his life when Jax suffered from insomnia had been when ... he was wrong about something.

No matter how he tried to justify the harsh words he launched at Addi, Jax knew—he was wrong. She had told him she had cared about him, even as a teen. A catch in his throat startled Jax. It would take a machete to clear away the maze of confused thoughts wound tightly around his mind.

So many questions still about his father's dealings with old

Vic. And Chase? And the guilt that he should have been carrying around all these years but instead had selfishly left behind.

How could he begin to address his feelings for Addi with still so much left to unravel about the past?

He began to walk again, Olive at his heels. He picked up a length of driftwood and tossed it into the surf. She looked up at him with an expression that asked, "Who, me?"

"Dogs are supposed to go running into the water, aren't they?"

Olive turned her face to the sea and then back up to him. Her forehead shifted, questioning him, and he grimaced. "I'll take that as a no." They walked on. He still had much to learn about how women thought—even the canine variety.

Addi hadn't shown up for work in two days. "She's taking some much needed vacation," Lily had told him. His sister's look of disgust wasn't lost on him. He imagined Lily had already given Addi an I-told-you-so speech.

What did he expect? That Addi would absorb all he had said to her, in the accusing tone he had used—he really needed to learn when the courtroom voice was creeping in—and show up the next day lighthearted and smiling, as if none of it had mattered?

Lily had barely spoken to him either, except to tell him to get Olive home at a decent time. His little sister had turned into the matriarch overnight, and though he welcomed it, the thought frightened him too. In some ways, he was beginning to believe he had long ago ceded the first-born duties to her.

Wasn't fair, but she had inherited their mother's strong fist when it came to running their family life, so he had let her. A lot easier than having to deal with family drama all the way from Chicago.

But how much did you miss?

He sifted through his thoughts. Leaving Lily to make all the decisions where their mother was concerned—since he was so far away—was an excuse. Maybe one lacking in fairness. Jax could not shake the sense that Lily had made his life easier by stepping in where he had not.

Olive sat up, her ears on alert. A bevy of fat sandpipers toddled in low tide, like drunkards. Jax stopped, waiting to see if the animal with a heart of gold and willpower to match was about to step out of character.

The tide receded, and those sandpipers ran up the shore in exaggerated fashion. Olive whined. She jerked forward then stopped, as if trying to rein herself in.

But then ... she couldn't stop herself anymore. Olive took off running down the beach, sending those overfed birds scattering in the air above her. Jax shook his head, chuckling. He could've stayed out here all day watching this nonsense.

His phone buzzed and his smile faded. His boss was on the line. He cleared his throat.

"Good morning, Brock."

"I caught you. Excellent."

"Yes, sir."

"I'm going to have Hannah send a file over for the Kinsey case. We've talked about this one, so I know you're familiar with the particulars."

"I believe I am."

"Good. Now, have it read thoroughly by the time you return. Perhaps on the plane home. I'll need you to be up to speed by the time your flight lands at O'Hare. I trust you can handle that?"

Even two weeks ago, a call like this would turn up a flame that already burned. Jax's nights and weekends had begun to look an awful like his days, and he had found that the more files were added to his caseload, the more synergy was created to absorb all that information.

Until now. After hanging up, Jax whistled for Olive to come. Together they moseyed back up the path to the house on the hill. The ocean had done its job, elevating his serotonin levels, but the call from Chicago had tempered its effects.

As did all those long and lingering thoughts of Addi. More so. She had been pretty when they were kids, though he had been slow to notice. When other guys in school started hitting on her, he went a little berserk. Took it out on her by ignoring her in their senior year, as if somehow that would teach her not to be so ... becoming.

What a dolt.

He wasn't surprised when she declared she would be marrying Bradford. Mad as heck, yes. But surprised? Not at all. And he had fully expected that if he were ever to cross paths with the beautiful Addison Barrett again, she'd be the glowing mother of three.

Thank the good Lord that was not the case.

Bottom line: He missed her. Jax flinched again at the memory of his harsh words. In essence, he had been ... a complete jerk.

Now if an opposing attorney had leveled such an accusation, he would have worn it as a badge of honor. Maybe even paraded it around the office. But today it hung like a scarlet letter around his neck available for all to see.

He and Olive jogged up the path to the house. When they arrived on the porch, he filled up her water dish with the hose to rehydrate. Jax had been asking himself exactly why he had been such a jerk to Addi, as if there would be some logical explanation. Truth was, he had been in the wrong about Chase

... that night of the fire ... and frankly, not giving one whit about what had been going on around him on that fateful night—and the many days and weeks afterward.

Lily opened the screen door and stepped out onto the porch, hardly acknowledging Jax's presence. She squatted down to greet Olive when the old dog approached her with water dripping from her hairy jaw. "Well, good morning, sunshine. You're a sight for sore eyes, yes you are."

He controlled the eye roll attempting to burst forth.

His sister stood, glanced out to the west, then zeroed in on him. "She's still not here, by the way."

"Thank you for the news update.

"You're an idiot."

"And you weren't asked."

Lily crossed her arms, the line of her mouth grim. She took a seat in the rocking chair and elicited a sigh. "It's like history repeating itself, isn't it? You and Addi, or lack thereof?"

"Whatever do you mean, dear sister?"

"It's not funny, you know, this yanking people's emotions around for sport. Maybe it's time we all start fresh. Get on with it already."

"Meaning?"

"I'm moving home, Jax. It's time for me to figure out where I should be headed during this next phase of my life. And I think you should too before you break anymore hearts."

"I'll ignore that last bit of commentary. But what you're saying is you are open to selling this house? The business?"

Lily smirked. "Leave it to a lawyer to twist my words like that."

Jax sputtered.

"But yes. I think we should sell it all and get on with our lives. Lucky will have the hardest time with it, I think, but

Nate's built his own compound—just needs a woman and kids to fill it. And I guess we'll have to find Chase to sign off on things, but my gut tells me that won't be a problem. Well, getting him to sign won't be a problem."

"Finding him might though."

"Right."

"May I ask ... why the change of heart, Lily?"

"Because I'm tired. Up until now, most of the decision making has fallen to me."

"It didn't have to be that way."

Her chin shot up, the angles in her jaw sharp. "Oh no? What way could it have been, brother?"

He ran his hand across the back of his neck. Getting into a scramble with Sergeant Lily wasn't on his agenda today. She had this idea in her head that burdens had been dumped on her, which was hardly the case. She could have moved out of the way a hundred times. But hadn't she chosen to stay?

When he didn't respond, she clucked her tongue, followed by a sigh. She found her way to one of the rockers and sat back, closing her eyes.

Olive looked up at him with a look that said, *You gonna just stand there and take that from her?* Of course, that was his interpretation ...

Lily cut in before he could gather his thoughts, her voice wistful. "Sure would've been nice to have a sister."

Have two Lilies in his life? He thought better than to voice what popped into his head just then. Instead, "What about four loving brothers?"

She sighed. "I know you're joking, and I know you think I'm a 'sergeant.'" She air quoted that without opening her eyes. "But decision-making was built into me from birth. That and justice-seeking. I couldn't avoid this part of me if I tried."

166

So she was basically agreeing with him ...

"But," she continued, "it would have been nice to have a sister to bounce things off, to not have to bear the weight of every decision. It's not like I think I have a lock on what is always the best decision. It's just ... someone has to make them."

"What about me? Or Nate or any of the others?"

She waved her hand in the air in that discounting way of hers. "Please."

Lily lay there, her back against the old rocker, a frown tugging at her mouth. A pang of sadness pulled inside of his chest, and sarcasm no longer had a place there. Remorse of lost years, the kind that had been pushing him through the week and had stopped dead center in front of him. He snapped another look at his sister. She barked orders from her sick bed last week, but now?

Lily looked as if she wanted to give up.

Questions stirred within him. Though she didn't realize it, he, too, had burdens to bear. "Lily?"

"Hmm?"

He touched her hand, and she opened one eye.

"I want to talk to you about something ... maybe you have some insight you could share with me."

"Go on." Her voice sounded anything but empathetic.

He took a seat in the other rocker. Olive padded over and put her head on his knee, as if offering support. "It's about the fire that happened when we were kids, at the old hardware store."

"What about it?"

"Vic made some outrageous claim yesterday, when I met him for coffee."

"You had coffee with Vic?" Her eyes were closed. "I can't

picture that."

"He said"—Jax took a breath, not sure how wise it would be to repeat what the old man told him—"he said Dad started the fire for the insurance money. That he paid him off."

"That old weasel."

"So you don't think it's true either?"

"I know it's not."

Jax watched his sister, his antennae up. "What aren't you telling me?"

Lily opened her eyes now. She sat up and linked her hands, stretching her arms forward. "How many years of college have you had? And law school too?"

"What does that have—"

She let out an unladylike groan. "There was no insurance money because Dad did not want to implicate Chase—or you."

"You heard about that, huh?"

She rolled her eyes. "Mom and Dad paid the price for both of you dimwits."

Jax stared after her, mouth open. Finally, "How do you know that?"

"Because Mom told me. She confided in me a lot."

"So you were privileged to be in the know about things that even I, as the oldest, was unaware."

"Sometimes I wished she wouldn't," she shot back. "Frankly, you should have been aware."

His mouth opened again, instinct telling him to shoot back a barbed response. But hadn't he just spent the past twenty-four hours in self-loathing over the very same thing with Addi? The bottom line was all was not as it seemed for the past dozen years. And he had happily allowed that to happen, while others paid for his mistakes.

Jax leaned his head against the back of the rocker. "Lily? Why did Mom tell you all that?"

"I think it's because she needed to confide in someone, and she knew that if she asked me not to say anything, I wouldn't."

"To understand, Dad knew I'd shirked my responsibility where Chase was concerned, and he never said anything? Never kicked my butt?"

"He didn't want you to miss out on the big world you were poised to conquer."

"He did give me quite the lecture before I got on the plane. I had packed my whole world into a suitcase and backpack, and he told me never to forget where I came from or who I was. I think he repeated a Bible verse too." He stared off into the field. "Sure wish I had written that down."

Lily considered Jax for several long seconds but didn't say a thing.

"I thought he was just giving me Dad-isms."

His sister exhaled a small laugh, something he found oddly comforting.

Somewhere in his head, mixed in with case law and statutes, the pastor's words from the service the other day were embedded. *Let the Lord determine your steps ...* He pressed his lips together, meditating on the words that had popped into his mind again and made a note to look them up soon. It wouldn't surprise him if his father would have admonished him with them as well.

Something out in the meadow caught Olive's attention, and she bounded off the porch. He lunged forward, but Lily's hands caught him. "Let her go. She needs to go chase squirrels for a while."

"Lily?"

"Hmm?"

"Why do you really think Chase hasn't shown up around here?"

"Like everyone else, at first, I thought it was grief. We all have our own way of dealing with it, and until it happens, one might not know what that is."

"But now?"

"Oh, Jax. I think ..."

"That Chase is ticked at me and couldn't face having to deal with my presence and his grief."

"You said it better than I could."

"I tried to find him yesterday, to apologize. Even went into the police station."

"And?"

"All Nate would say was that he didn't want to be found."

Lily sighed. Olive returned, panting. She found a sunny spot on the porch and curled up in it, but not before giving Jax one long look with her good eye. A small whine escaped her, but she settled into her curled up pose, tucking her chin into her body.

"She's been pretty mopey lately," Lily said.

"I'm gonna miss her."

"Will wonders never cease."

He swallowed back a retort. "She'll be happier here with you though."

Lily peered at Jax.

"What?"

"Mom fostered her with the idea of finding her a home, eventually. And that day has come."

"You're ... not serious."

Lily frowned. "Thought that would have made you pleased."

"What ... what do you know about these people?" His

windpipe constricted. He had come to regard Olive as his mother's pet, inextricably intertwined with her memory.

"Not a whole lot, I'm afraid. I had hoped Terry Schwartz could take her—she's a local foster mom with a great rep—but she's been dealing with a cancer diagnosis." She sighed. "So she recommended a family from down south a bit. Sounds like they'll take great care of her."

Jax glanced at Olive, curled up between them now. From what he had heard, she had been uprooted more than once before. And now it was about to happen again.

She should be on some distant shore, drinking a mai tai by the sea. Instead, Addi sat in the town's only dimly lit coffee house, a place with admittedly the worst coffee in town, poring over her mother's favorite cookbook. The pages were dog-eared and splotched from recipe testing, but she didn't care. In fact, those things had become more evidence of her mother's ways—reminders of who she was and would forever be inside Addi's heart.

It felt strange to be in such close proximity to her father's store, yet have no intention of going inside. She had originally planned to work today, despite their come-to-Jesus talk yesterday, but her father had sent her a text saying he wasn't ready to see her yet.

First Jax had blamed her for decisions of the past and now her father.

"Hello, Addi."

She looked up. "Bradford?"

"Still obsessed with cookbooks, I see."

"Always." She closed the cover and gestured to an open seat next to her. "Would you like to sit down?"

He sidled a look at the door, then pulled out the chair. "For a minute, sure."

The man sitting across from her elicited nothing from her other than, perhaps, brotherly love. No attraction. No heightened tension. He was just a guy she once knew.

"You're looking good," he said.

"And you as well."

From what she remembered, Bradford had found someone else to marry shortly after their breakup. Then he and his new wife moved about twenty minutes away to a posh little town with wine-tasting rooms and high-end boutiques. By the looks of his full face and dad bod, she guessed they had added to their family by now.

She fought back a tickle of a smile. "How are you these days?"

"Great. Carrie and I have a full house now."

"Congratulations. How many kids ... two?"

He held up four fingers.

"Oh ... my ... word."

"Saltwater is the only place I can get some peace and quiet for a few minutes." He chuckled, his shoulders bouncing. "This place has terrible coffee, but I make it work."

She held up a cup. "I hear you. The chai tea isn't too awful. Place has a good vibe though."

"Eh, I guess." He sipped his coffee and looked around the room. "This beats unpacking boxes."

"Oh, so you moved recently?"

"Nah. Carrie likes to buy toys and things online. My job is to put them all together."

Addi laughed.

He eyed her, his smile warm. "I owe you a huge thank you."

She straightened. "Oh really? What for?"

"For dumping me."

Addi's shoulders deflated. "I wouldn't call it that."

"Oh no?" Both of his brows lifted. "Said you couldn't marry me, so I'd call that a dumping."

"It wasn't you."

"I know, I know—it's not you, it's me." He clucked his tongue. "I've been watching *Seinfeld* reruns."

"Bradford, I'm perfectly serious."

He brushed the air with his hands. "Everybody around here knows I was the rebound guy."

"That's not true!" Addi's heart sank. So much for her feelings for Jax being a well-kept secret in a small town.

"Sure. Whatever." He scooched into his chair. "All I wanted to say is, well, I'm a happy guy." He slapped his gut with his hands. "My wife feeds me well, and I can't imagine being married to anyone else. So, you did me a favor."

What was she to say to that? You're welcome?

Before she came up with an answer, the smudgy glass front door opened and Bradford spun around again. Jumpy guy, that one. He muttered something under his breath that she couldn't quite make out. Sounded like *just my luck...*

Addi raised her gaze to the door where Jax stood with Olive by his side. Her heart leapt and fell in one swift second, leaving the dull thud of a heavy heartbeat in her chest.

"Look who's back in town," Bradford said when Jax approached. He dropped his sights to Olive. "Didn't know they allowed dogs in this establishment."

Addi gestured for Olive to come to her. "Trust me. No one cares."

"Hello, Bradford."

Addi cut in. "Jax's mom passed away recently. He's been here to pay his respects."

Bradford nodded an acknowledgment. "And then it's back to the big city, I suppose."

"Afraid so." Jax cleared his throat, but made no move to sit. "I won't keep you two, but thought Addi might want to say hello to her favorite one-eyed pet."

Bradford frowned. He scanned Olive's face. "Would you look at that ... only one eye on her. That's a big shame."

Addi shrugged. "She gets along just fine and doesn't milk it, though she could if she wanted to." She said all this while giving the pup an abundance of pets.

"Looks like she wants to go home with you," Jax said.

Addi sighed. "Aw, I wish she could, but my landlord would have my head." She gave Jax a casual glance. "I made the exception recently, but only for a little while. Sure wish I could keep her though."

He nodded, his expression unsettled, as it should be. If it weren't for Olive being with him, she might not have even given Jax much of a greeting. He had all but blamed her for Chase's disappearance. She had carried the weight of that secret for a long time and didn't appreciate his condemnation. But she was not about to make a scene in front of her old fiancé.

"We should go." He glanced down. "Come, Olive."

Addi's throat caught. Likely, this would be the last time she would see Jax before he left. "Wait." She reached for Olive's collar and put her face close to the dog's. "Take care of yourself, sweet girl."

After they had left, she could hardly keep the sadness out of her expression, though she surely tried. Bradford kept her occupied with chatter about his kids and soccer and the truck he'd just bought. Then he downed the last of his coffee and stood. "Sure was nice running into you, Addi. Say hi to your dad. Always liked him."

Sure you did. Because he didn't hate you. You would have kept me close to Saltwater.

She pasted on the brightest of smiles. "Thanks. I will. Bye, Bradford."

He left her alone, the shop nearly empty, the place smelling of burned coffee beans. Her cell phone rang, and Lily's name flashed on the screen. But she turned off the ringer and slid it into her bag.

Everyone around her seemed to have made decisions that moved them forward in life. Even Bradford. Maybe it's time she did too. Addi made a mental note to call Pastor Simon first thing in the morning.

She knew.

Jax picked up the pace on his hike back to the house. Addi obviously knew Olive was being shipped off to some other family's home. He could tell by the tear-jerking expression on her face when she had kissed the pup goodbye. There was no other reason for that display, right? He swallowed back disappointment. Another secret she'd been keeping from him ...

"Where've you been?" Lily looked ready to pick a fight standing there with a fist on her hip.

He dropped his keys onto his mother's farmhouse table. "Not now, Lily."

She followed after him. "You know the foster couple will be here soon to pick up Olive and you took off anyway. What's wrong with you?"

He swung around, not wanting to make nice right now. "I wanted Addi to have a chance to say goodbye to Olive."

"Addi?" Lily shrank back, giving him a side eye. "You wanted Addi to say goodbye to 'Olive'?" She air quoted the dog's name. He was beginning to hate seeing those air quotes!

"Don't read something into this that's not there. I've got emails to answer and an important phone call to make." He started up the stairs, his shoulders tense. "Call me when they get here."

Upstairs, he shut his bedroom door and fired up his iPad. The work had begun to pile up in a way that could very well be unmanageable if he didn't start addressing some of it now. Tory had sent him three emails and left him one very long phone message. He closed his eyes and squared himself to drag his mind away from personal issues and back to the work at hand.

The sound of the doorbell pulled him out of his work. It felt like hours had passed, when really, it had only been forty-five minutes. He scowled.

Downstairs, an old couple with graying hair and kind smiles sat in the kitchen. The woman's hand rested on Olive's head, who incidentally, seemed to be lapping it up.

Not the kind of people he could easily find fault with. Still, he fought off a wresting in his heart.

"Doreen, Bertram, this is my brother, Jax."

He offered them a hello. Olive broke free of his new foster mom and trotted over to him. She bumped her noggin into his hand, as if to say, *Your turn now,* and he crouched down. A lump in his throat thickened.

"So I've told you about the medicine you'll need to give Olive," Lily was saying, "to keep her remaining eye healthy ..."

His sister yarned on with advice, but all he could see was Olive's watchful gaze. He patted her head again then stood.

"Come here, sugar." The old woman rooted around for something in her oversized bag. She pulled out a miniature hat, put it on Olive's head, and strapped it around her chin. "There. Now no one can see that nasty place where your eye once was. Covers it right up."

He cast a look at Lily, but his sister had this way of putting on a bright smile in the worst of circumstances. His experience drilling the truth out of witnesses didn't help him much when it came to his sister's carefully crafted ways.

But, c'mon, did she not also think that woman was absurd?

After a few minutes of polite banter, Bertram stood. "It's time to go, Doreen. Say your goodbyes, everyone."

Lily hesitated. She swallowed, keeping her gaze from Jax. Olive padded over to him, swiped a paw on his jeans and let out a whine. The dam in his throat was about to burst. He bent to say his goodbyes, and as he did, she leapt up and kissed him square on the mouth. Several slobbery kisses. Instead of drawing back in horror, tears rolled down his cheeks. For one quiet moment, he shut his eyes.

Bertram cleared his throat.

Jax took a deep breath. He bent his knees and scooped up Olive like a baby in his arms, her tail and paws flailing about in the air. Olive leaned her head against his chest as if to say, *It's about time!* "Sorry, folks," Jax said, "but Olive will be staying with me after all."

Doreen's mouth popped open and she elicited a gasp. Her husband frowned. "Then why'd we come all this way?"

Jax pulled a large bill out of his pants pocket and handed it to the man. "For your troubles." He turned and walked toward the living room now, Olive still secure in his arms, then he swung the front door open wide and stepped aside. "Thanks again for coming."

The old couple scuttled out onto the porch, both muttering to each other. Jax didn't dare look at Lily, who no doubt was seething at his sudden take-charge attitude. To smooth things over, later he would stop by the store and pick up her favorite bottle of wine. Chardonnay? Pinot grigio?

While he stood there debating over what kind of wine would make her happy, Lily lunged for him. She whipped the hat off Olive's head and stepped outside, hurrying up to the passenger side of the car. "Here, take this," she called out to Doreen. "We won't be needing it!"

Then she turned back around, smacking her hands together like she had just bid good riddance to something. She climbed the porch steps to where Jax stood, still clinging to Olive, and leveled a big, fat grin at him.

"I'm guessing you approve."

Lily nodded, her eyes filling with tears.

"Oh, now, don't you get started." Jax tried his best to give her a scolding gaze, but it didn't work. Lily lunged at him, tears flowing out of her. She hugged both him and Olive tightly, snotty sniffles in the crook of his neck.

He pulled away, trying not to laugh. "Okay, all right. Fine. Fine."

"I'm so, so happy, Jax. You have no idea."

He returned her smile, happy to have made the decision to keep Olive for himself. Now, if only he could figure out how to get Addi back ...

He quirked a look at his sister. "Where can I find a hardware store around here?"

Lily gave him a puzzled frown.

"No, not Vic's place. Another one."

She bit her lip as if thinking. "There are a couple of big box places twenty minutes away."

"Great. Okay if I borrow your wheels?"

She handed him the key and tilted her head to the side, a smile lingering. "What are you cooking up now, dear brother?"

He grabbed the key while still cradling the pup and dashed a kiss on her temple. "You'll see." Then he put Olive on the ground and together, they slipped out the door.

Chapter Ten

For all Addi knew, Jax was long gone back to Chicago and his fancy penthouse overlooking all that water. Mercifully, Lily had kept mum about her brother's plans, but she had told Addi to take a leave of absence from working at the doggy daycare. Addi took her up on that offer. Thankfully, she had savings. And why wouldn't she when she hadn't really gone anywhere for most of her life?

Maybe that would not be changing anytime soon, but some things might.

Addi clicked *submit* on the application in front of her. She'd never done something so ... so ... rash in her entire life. But she knew if she didn't take this risk now, she never would. And she would grow old in Saltwater Beach with nothing but a dingy hardware store to her name.

Speaking of which, it hadn't taken long for her father to ask her to come back.

"I need you, Addi," was all he said, and she agreed to help him today.

The sun was working its way toward the west, still keeping

JULIE CAROBINI

the day's air comfortable. She stepped outside in the warmth and hopped on her bike, careful to avoid riding past the Cooper home on her way to the store. She wasn't ready to face seeing the place just yet.

She parked her bike on the rack on the Main Street sidewalk just as Pastor Simon exited the hardware store. "Afternoon, Addi," he said.

"Hello, Pastor." He wasn't carrying a bag. "Didn't you find what you were looking for?"

He grinned. "I found exactly what I needed."

She gave him a quizzical look.

Pastor Simon leaned forward and lowered his voice. "Thank you for the phone chat the other day."

She bit her lip. "I'm sorry I never stopped in to see you. I truly meant to."

He lifted his hand to stop her. "You have your own life to live, my dear. I know how much you care for your father—it shows. I appreciated our talk."

Her face warmed. "Me as well." Addi had never been publicly transparent with all she felt about the difficulties with her mom's health and her dad's inability to cope. Most of the time, she wasn't aware of how deeply affected she'd become. But Pastor Simon had managed to draw thoughts out of her that could be exposed, addressed, and prayed over.

"You will be happy to learn that your father has agreed to attend counseling sessions with me. Been after him for some time, as you know."

"Really? Already?" A catch in her throat surprised her. "I appreciate how much you've been after my father lately. Thank you so much."

"Just a shepherd going after his lost one."

Tears made good on their threat. Addi threw her arms around her pastor and gave him a squeeze. "Bless you."

After he left, she entered the store, her heart lighter. She'd done what she could to avoid thinking about Jax back in Chicago and instead focused on moving forward in her own life, whatever that might look like. Knowing that someone was watching out for her father gave her the kind of peace that had long eluded her.

"You're here."

Addi slid her cross-body purse off and into a drawer behind the counter. "That I am," she said to her father. "Would you like to take a break?"

"Sure thing. The rush is long past ... might even close her up early."

Her dad's eyes drooped, the bags beneath them appearing heavier than she'd seen before. He sniffled, and she darted a concerned look at him. "Are you sick?"

Quickly, he shook his head. "Nope. Never felt better."

"Well, okay, then."

"Addi? I'm ..."

"Yes?"

He closed his mouth, frowning, the wrinkles in his forehead deep and jagged looking. "I just want to say that, well, I'm sorry for barking at you the other day. Perhaps I have been unfair to you."

"Yes, you have been unfair."

"I, uh, have been an ornery cuss." He raised his chin, as if owning up to what he'd just admitted to. "Not proud of it."

She nodded her acknowledgment.

"And I just want to say"—he flashed a pained look at her— "I am very glad you did not marry that Bradford fella."

She tilted her head. "Whoa. Where did that come from?"

"Lots of memories have been dredged up lately."

"Hmm. True. As I recall, you were pretty mad when I broke it off with him."

Her father pursed his lips. "I was wrong."

Addi had mistaken the expression on her father's face for illness when she had first walked into the store, but now she understood that what she saw on his face was remorse. It pained her.

Still, remorse had its purpose, for all of them. As an adult, she came to recognize that her father had long struggled with the direction his life had taken—including the results of his own choices. She had too.

"I forgive you, Daddy."

"Well, then. Good."

She gave him a peck on the cheek, unwilling to let bitterness take root. "Come by the apartment tonight after work. I'll make you some of Mama's rigatoni."

"Not that gluten-free stuff, I hope."

She clucked a laugh. "Fine. I'll make you some gluten-laden noodles in one pot and my favorite noodles in another."

He kissed her on the head and gave her shoulders a squeeze that lingered. "I've never told you this, but I like when you bake that strange stuff. Reminds me of your mother."

Addi tucked those words in her heart, knowing how much they would always mean to her.

"Welp," he said. "I'm gonna head home. Close up when you're ready."

The old bell on the front door chimed, indicating that closing time would not be coming just yet. She shooed him away and moved to a spot behind the counter to help their customer.

"Hello, may I—"

Jax stood in front of the counter. Her gaze found its way up his jean-clad self and staring straight into those penetrating eyes of his.

"Addi."

"You're still ... here."

"I am."

By his side, Olive whined. Addi tore her gaze away from Jax's chiseled face. "Hello to you, too, Olive darling." The animal's mouth popped open. If that didn't look exactly like a smile ...

Jax broached first, a certain pleading in his stare, a gradual dip in his brows. "Can we go somewhere and ... talk?"

Tempting. A beat passed, though, and she shook her head no just as the door opened. A woman wandered in and made a beeline for the paint tools aisle. "I'm on duty. Just arrived a few minutes ago, actually."

He didn't answer her right away, but continued to consider her, his lips pressed together. Finally, "Understood."

Jax didn't turn to leave, however. Instead, he glanced around, looking very much like the younger version of himself Addi had always remembered, even long after he had moved on with his life.

She resisted the urge to reach out and caress his face. What good would it do to drag her emotions back into something that would only re-break her heart? How many times could she do that to herself?

The deep tone of his voice awoke her from her musings. "I'm sorry I hurt you."

She met his gaze. A moment ago, he may have resembled a teenager, but right now? He was all man—smoldering, strong, but contrite and directing every ounce of his attention on her. Addi nodded, sensing her resolve melt away.

Jax took a step closer. "I want to show you something—"

A woman's voice interrupted him. "Excuse me? Could you tell me where the cutting-in tools are?"

Addi broke eye contact with Jax, hard as that was. "Of course." She looked toward the woman and stepped out from behind the counter. "Follow me."

She could have told the customer what aisle number to go to, but leading her there would give Addi the chance to break free of Jax's hold on her—even if for only a minute. She could guide a customer to whatever they needed without much thought, giving her ample time to get her bearings.

The woman picked up the tool she needed and followed Addi back to the counter. Jax stayed put, he and Olive like permanently installed statues. After her customer had gone, Jax scooped Olive into his arms like an infant. He moved close to the counter again.

"Look at the tag on her collar," he said.

Addi reached for the dog-bone shaped tag. "Olive ... Cooper?" She snapped a look at Jax. "That's an out-of-area phone number on there. You— you're adopting her?"

He leaned across the counter. "I am."

"But I thought Lily was looking for a foster ..."

A smile grew on his face. "That fell through."

A mixture of relief and sadness filtered through her. She cast a longing look at the odd pair—a one-eyed dog without a home and the penthouse-dwelling lawyer who never cared for animals ...

Gently, he set Olive on the ground and stood back up to face her, an intensity overtaking his face. "Come with us."

Addi's mind swirled with protests and questions. What was he asking? "I—"

"I'm sorry for being such a hothead, a jerk!" He blurted. "I take full responsibility for my actions, both in the past and now. Ah, Addi ... you were *always* the best thing to ever happen to me."

"I— it's fine. It's all in the past, Jax."

"I should not have blamed you for Chase's disappearance." He ran a hand through his hair, a look of horror in his expression. "Can you ever forgive me for being such a ... a dolt? I should have thought, both then and now, about all you had to face with your family."

She swallowed. First her father, now Jax. If only she felt fully ready to shake off the remnant of blame that she continued to hold on to. "Really, Jax. It's okay. After thinking more about it, how could I blame you for your reaction?"

Jax's brows dipped further. "There's more I need to say to you." He bit his bottom lip and looked upward, as if the words he needed were hanging from those rafters. He dropped his chin and caught her gaze. "Addi, I want to tell you why my engagement ended."

"You— you don't have to. Really."

"Yes, I do."

She nodded. "Okay. Just a minute." Addi stepped over to the front door, turned the sign to Closed, and pulled down a shade on the long, windowed door. "Let's walk."

Jax, Addi, and Olive ducked down the alleyway behind Main Street, following it all the way to the beach. Without saying a thing, they took off their shoes and left them near a lifeguard tower. Olive ran off toward the shore, and they followed behind, walking along in the still salt air.

Jax interrupted the tension between them. "I didn't end the engagement. Mara did."

She had heard rumors it was an ugly scene—Chase had laughed once and said she should have been there—but really, no one had ever spilled actual details. At least, not to her. "I'm sorry."

"Don't be. I deserved it. She, uh, left me the night before the wedding."

"Oh. How awful."

"Brutal, I know. I remember asking her if there was someone else, and she said, 'Yes, I believe so.'"

"Oh ..."

"When I asked her his name, she looked me in the eye and said, 'I think we both know, Jax, that it's not *his* name, but *hers* —you're still in love with a girl from your past.'"

Addi gasped. "What? No, Jax. We-we hadn't seen each other in ... years." She crossed her arms. "I don't understand."

"I believed it was crazy talk too, and I said as much. Thoughts of the past snaked through my head as she stood there, accusing me of loving somebody else." He looked out to sea, as if reliving that painful time. His voice had turned quiet. "How could I be in love with someone I hadn't spoken to in years? Ludicrous. Right?"

Addi couldn't answer that. Only now, when faced with past truths, could she see just how poorly she had moved on after Jax left and stayed away so long. She dug a toe into wet sand and idly made some loop-de-loops with it. "I'm sure you told her that was impossible."

"I tried. But all she did was look at me and shake an old teddy bear she had found in my apartment, and say, 'Really, Jax?'"

"The teddy bear?"

He sighed. "That last night at the fair, you'd won that bear for me."

"I remember. Wow. I can't believe you kept it so long."

"Yeah. Kind of my own mascot, if you will. Took it to

college, then law school, and it cheered me on from my book-shelf while studying to take the bar in two states." He was smiling now, though shyly, a glimpse into yesterday. "I guess I always thought of it as a good luck charm."

"But surely you told her that's all it was."

"She saw through me. Apparently, I barked at her when she tried to give it away to charity, though I don't remember that." He shrugged and began to walk again, following along behind Olive. "Chase had met Mara once. He had been out to see Chicago and needed a place to stay. He and I had drifted apart, well, I understand better why now. Anyway, Mara told him about the bear incident—I think she was just making fun of me at the time—but apparently, he spilled it that you'd won it for me ..."

"Oh."

He stopped and crossed his arms, taking in the undulating waves spread out before them. "She told me it all started making sense to her then, that I was still in love with my high-school crush."

Addi centered her gaze on the ocean. She could not look at him now—would not. "I never knew you had a crush on me."

"That's because I could never admit it, even to myself. Your friendship was everything to me. All those years of hanging out until long past dark, digging moats and castles during summers, and then all of a sudden—"

"I grew up. We both did."

"Yeah. Other guys were noticing you. It made me crazy. And then Bradford? Don't get me started."

"You were kind of distant to me after that. Mean, even."

His breath rushed out of him. "I'm sorry."

"You don't have to say any more, Jax."

"Let me get it out, okay?" He exhaled again. "Chase and I

had a big fight over what he said to Mara. I told him to mind his own business, and he just took off, back to Saltwater." He hooked eyes with hers. "We haven't spoken since. I honestly believed this disappearing act of his had something to do with that argument."

"That he was avoiding you."

"Right."

"And maybe he was, but for an altogether different reason."

A whoosh of a breath left him. "You mean the fire and his ... guilt."

"Yes." She sighed and stayed quiet a moment, then gently, "Did Mara really believe that an old teddy bear was standing between the two of you?"

"I challenged her with that same question. Apparently, she had let it fester, never saying much about it to me until that night. We had a hotel full of guests ... it was a difficult time, to say the least."

"What did she say when you challenged her?"

"She looked me right in the eyes and said, 'You don't remember, do you?' I had no idea what she was talking about, but the night before, right after she'd told me she loved me on the phone, I said, 'I love you too, Addi.'"

She blinked. The words she had so longed to hear floated on the air between them, as if looking for a safe place to land.

He continued. "In the end, she said she would not marry someone who had not let go of the past, that it was unfair to both of us. And that was that."

Jax stopped. He pivoted so that Addi could no longer keep her gaze centered on the sea. She either had to look at him or step away. She allowed her eyes to trail upward until her gaze rested squarely on his. He closed the space between them until she could hear the cadence of his breathing. "I knew she was right, even then. I may have moved on in my career, but with Mara, I was holding something back. She sensed it. And I guess I didn't want to admit it when I got here. Especially assuming you had moved on."

He reached for her hand, threading his fingers with hers, but no longer spoke.

Olive was in sight, just over Jax's shoulder. So Addi closed her eyes to the lull of the sea. Everything in this moment could have been described as perfect.

But ... she couldn't just up and change her mind on a whim. That's all this was, right? A man's reaction to tragedy ... nostalgia ... thoughts of *what if*. If she were to drop everything and follow Jax to the city, she would be jumping from one unknown to another.

"Come with me," he whispered.

Addi licked her lips. She connected her gaze with his. "In many ways," she said, "I feel like the female version of Rip Van Winkle. Like I've just woken up from the longest nap ever."

A slight grin appeared on his face.

"And now I suppose it's time for me to figure out what my future looks like."

"Figure it out with me. And Olive."

Tears threatened for the second time today, and Addi sensed they shimmered enough that Jax could see them too. "Truthfully, Jax? I still feel a bit like a pariah around here. The girl who kept a secret she had no business keeping."

He shook his head vehemently. "No."

She drew taller, lifting her chin. "I am working on some plans I haven't shared yet with anyone, not even my father. Or Lily."

His eyes dulled some. "And what you're saying is, they don't include me."

JULIE CAROBINI

"I'm sorry, but no. I think it's just too much for us to overcome."

* * *

"I'm glad you finally said yes to this excursion," Lily said.

Addi smiled. After Jax and Olive left town, Lily had left multiple messages for her. She had not been in the mood for phone calls but finally relented, picking up on her friend's fourth try.

"Don't hang up!" she'd said. "I've booked us a spa day down south, and I'm not taking no for an answer."

Two more days had passed since that phone call, and the two were heading down the 101 freeway in Lily's truck. Addi examined her fingernails and admitted the truth to herself: Her cuticles hadn't been addressed in months. It was time. "Thanks again for the invitation." Addi relaxed against the headrest. "Can't remember the last time I did something like this."

"Probably never!" Lily slid a look at Addi. "I'm so thankful for all you did to help me with tending to my mother's home and her memorial."

"It was my pleasure."

"Besides, I needed the break from all the quiet around the house now."

Addi knew that saying goodbye to Olive was harder for Lily than she'd once thought it would be. Animals had a way of burrowing so deeply into our lives that they left a gaping hole when they're gone. But Addi suspected that for Lily, saying goodbye to Jax was even harder.

As it was for her. Achingly so.

Addi glanced out the window, an ocean of blue stretching to the horizon. She fought off all thoughts of Jax and their reunion after all these years. At the moment, she wanted to think about anything ... anything but that. "Oh!" She turned to Lily. "Weren't we supposed to stop somewhere on the way down here?"

"Shoot. Yes." Lily sighed. "All that stuff in the back that has to go to Salvation Army. Will you remind me to swing by there on the way back into town?"

"Well, I've already failed at that once."

Lily laughed. "You didn't fail. I guess I was just too eager to get to our mani-pedi appointments!"

As they pulled into the sweeping entry of the Sea Glass Inn's parking lot, Addi promised to remind Lily to make the stop on their way home. A valet appeared on the driver's side and addressed Lily through the open window. "Welcome. Will you be checking in?"

Lily popped open her door and hopped down to the ground. "I wish! No, but we're here to visit the spa."

"Excellent." The valet tore off a ticket and handed it to Lily, while a second valet opened Adi's door and waited for her to exit the truck. "Enjoy your visit, ladies."

The lobby bustled with people, some in golf attire, others in business suits, and a few stragglers wearing coverups over swimwear. Addi spotted the concierge desk at the same time Lily did.

Lily approached a young woman at the concierge desk. "Good morning, Trace."

Trace smiled. "Oh, Lily! How nice to see you again."

Addi peered at her friend.

"What?" Lily said, with a shrug. "Can't a girl have her secrets?"

"A newbie, I presume?" Trace said, eyeing Addi. "You two ladies are in for a treat!" The woman wagged her head, smiling.

"The spa gets improvements every day it seems. I tell you, that place'll heal whatever ails you. Pinky promise."

Lily laughed. "Perfect. I think we both could use some of that right now."

Addi followed Lily down a long hall that turned toward beautiful glass doors. Inside, a palatial spa with soft lighting and clean, white furniture layered with linen welcomed them.

They were greeted by a receptionist. "May I help you?"

"We both have appointments for the works," Lily said.

Addi gasped. "That's far too generous. You said mani-pedis, and that's plenty."

"No, I said that to get you to come with me. You'll have a choice of services, but first massages!"

"Follow me, ladies." The receptionist led them to a smaller waiting room with glossy travel magazines and soothing music playing. It smelled like lemongrass and eucalyptus. Minutes later, they were each whisked away to private massage rooms.

An hour later, Lily found Addi laying in her robe by the adults-only spa pool. Addi opened one eye, shading her face with her hand. "I literally cannot move."

Lily laughed. "No, you don't want to move."

"Same difference."

"May I get you ladies anything to drink?" A male attendant asked.

Addi noticed Lily momentarily swoon over the muscle-blessed guy in the Hawaiian shirt before catching herself.

Lily said, "A couple of bottles of water would be amazing."

After he left, Addi quipped, "Sure you don't want to go over there and help him dig through the fridge?"

Lily slapped her arm. "Stop it."

Addi laughed. "Can't. Feels good to smile again."

"Looks good on you too."

Addi sat up. "Speaking of looking good, I made a hair appointment in the salon. There was one opening and I snagged it. Hope you don't mind."

"Oh, *sa-lone*, huh? Such a proper pronunciation for a beach girl. And no, I don't mind at all."

"Yes, well, that's how they say it at resorts. When in Rome ..."

"Ha ha. Okay. I'm having my brows waxed. Let's plan to meet in the cafe afterward. Sound good?"

Addi agreed and headed back inside to change before finding the hair salon, where she was led to a chair in front of a mirror framed with round lights. Her relaxed face looked back at her.

"Good afternoon," a woman with flowing red hair said. She floated a shiny cape in front of Addi and affixed it behind her neck. "I'm Priscilla. And who do I have the pleasure of meeting?"

"Addi Barrett. Happy to meet you, Priscilla."

Priscilla gently put her manicured hands on Addi's shoulders and smiled at her in the mirror. "What are we doing today?"

"Honestly? I'm not sure." She laughed a little self-consciously. "Isn't that kind of silly? I haven't thought much about that part, but maybe it's because I'm so relaxed from my massage."

Priscilla smiled. "Oh, I know how that is!"

"All I know is that I need ... change."

Any fear that the hairstylist would show annoyance over her indecision was quickly dashed. "Oh, darling, I know exactly what you mean." She patted both hands once on Addi's lapels. "Leave it to me."

Priscilla washed Addi's hair and gave her a head massage

that nearly lulled her to sleep. She wondered if her legs would have the ability to carry her out of the Sea Glass Inn when the time came—she was that relaxed.

Priscilla worked smoothing cream into Addi's hair and began to comb it straight. "Beautiful hair. You must take great care of it."

"Thank you. I try, but I rarely do anything other than blow it dry."

"You've got some nice curl in here. Have you ever thought of layering it to highlight those?"

She'd always thought of her hair as thick and unruly. But her mother had curls. Maybe all hers needed was a little encouragement.

"I haven't, but I think I'd like to try that."

"Wonderful! You could still flat iron them when you're in the mood for something different."

"Thank you for helping me see what I wanted, even when I didn't know myself."

"Aw, isn't that the way sometimes? We go along in life, doing the same thing over and over again, when suddenly someone makes a suggestion and a light goes off in our heads."

A montage of Addi's life popped into her head. Most days she went from her apartment to the doggy daycare to her father's shop and home again. Other than occasional walks on the beach, she could not think of one unplanned move she ever made.

Addi sighed and Priscilla's scissors stopped above her. "Everything all right?"

"I was just thinking I could use more of those lightbulb moments in my life."

A slow smile spread across Priscilla's face. Her fingers and scissors began moving again. "Do you ever pray?"

Addi's eyes met Priscilla's in the mirror. "Yes, I can honestly say that I do."

"But do you pray for yourself?"

Addi swallowed, not sure how to answer that. Did she? Her problems seemed so small compared to people suffering from illness, like her mother, Melanie Cooper ... even her father and his addictions.

Priscilla must have noticed her silence. "Listen," she said gently, "take it from someone who knows. If you confess the desires of your heart to God, he will listen."

"What if you're not sure what they are?"

"Give Him what you've got. Talk to him about the secret things you have in your heart. He'll take those thoughts and dreams and mold them into something altogether new. Much better than what you could dream up on your own." She winked, Addi catching sight of it in the mirror. "Trust me on this."

Later, when Lily spotted her in the hotel's cafe, her mouth dropped open. "Oh. My. Word!"

Addi shushed her, laughing and gesturing for her to sit down already.

Lily touched one of her curls, her eyes truly open wide. "Addi, you are the spitting image of your sweet mama."

Tears pooled in Addi's eyes. "I saw it too."

"Wow. I love it. How come you never wore it this way before?"

"You know, I've been asking myself that same question ever since I stepped out of the salon."

"Don't you mean *sa-lone*?"

"Ha. Yes. That too."

A waitress brought them menus and waters. "Here you are, ladies. I'll be back to get your order shortly."

"Lily, this has been an amazing day. I can't get over it." She sniffled, suddenly overcome by her friend's generosity, not to mention all Priscilla had given her to ponder.

"Oh, now, don't get all blubbery on me. My brows are already red from the waxing. How will I look with mascara running down my face too?"

"Like a clown, maybe?"

Lily spat out a laugh and slapped Addi playfully with her menu. "Stop that! You're running me from one emotion to the other. I can't take it!"

Addi laughed until she cried. She grabbed a napkin and dotted her eyes, then lightly blew her nose. "I've been thinking a lot about my life, how things haven't been all that smooth."

Lily reached out and patted her hand. "I know."

"Do you pray? I mean, for yourself? Your future?"

Lily seemed to think about that. "Well, I guess you could say that I pray in spite of myself." She sighed. "What I mean is, sometimes there's so much to pray for that I find myself stymied. But I know that's what I am to do, and I've truly seen God's blessings come from it."

Addi blinked rapidly, those tears pressing forward again.

"I didn't mean to make you cry!"

"It's fine, it's fine!" She plucked the napkin from her lap and attempted to dry her eyes with it. In her peripheral, she noticed two women walking nearby. One wore a sharp, red pantsuit, and the other a fitted sleeveless dress. The one in red stepped up to the table. "Hello again, Lily."

"Meg! How nice to see you. Meet my friend, Addi."

"Welcome, Addi," Meg said.

Lily turned to fill Addi in. "Meg's family owns the inn. And her friend Liddy is like her right hand or something."

Liddy laughed as Meg quipped, "She wishes."

Addi peered at Lily. Even though Trace at the concierge desk greeted her friend earlier, Addi really hadn't realized just how often Lily had frequented the inn.

"Are you enjoying your spa day, Addi?" Liddy asked.

"I am." She hoped her face didn't look too blotchy from all the tears. Addi cleared her throat. "It's a beautiful inn. I just had my hair done by Priscilla and I love it."

Meg smiled. "She's a gem. I'm so glad you caught her today."

Liddy slid into a chair and lowered her voice. "You know her honey's a billionaire, right?"

Lily leaned forward. "No way. And she cuts hair?"

Meg rolled her eyes and took the empty seat next to Liddy. "Priscilla is a dear friend of ours, and she likes to come in a few times per month. You're blessed to have gotten in to see her today."

Of all the days and all the times Priscilla could have come in, she chose today. A hardened section of Addi's heart softened some at the favor she'd been shown.

"I was just telling Addi how pretty her new hairstyle is," Lily said. "Quite the transformation!"

"Did you get it done for something special?" Liddy asked.

Lily butted in. "We really just came for some rest and rejuvenation after a few hard months."

Meg offered a sympathetic smile. "That's reason enough. But maybe a trip somewhere would help even more."

Liddy laughed. "Meg ... always ready to get on a plane and fly off to somewhere exotic at a moment's notice."

"Oh, hush." Meg smiled. "I do love my frequent flier miles though."

Lily turned to Addi. "Maybe traveling isn't such a bad idea.

If I wasn't so swamped, I would go with you. Why don't you consider it?"

"Me? I've hardly ever been out of Saltwater. Plus, I've never been on a plane."

"Why not?" Meg asked.

All three women waited for an answer.

"Well, maybe it's because ... I'm scared."

"Of flying?" Meg asked.

Liddy cut in. "Here we go."

Meg waved her away. "I love flying! I've seen the world that way. You'll love it—I promise."

Liddy chuckled. "See what I mean?"

After the women left, Lily and Addi stayed for lunch, lingering in the dining room.

"I've been thinking of what you told Liddy and Meg earlier," Lily said, "about being afraid. I just want to say that I hope I didn't ruin things between you and Jax."

"What? No. How do you mean?"

She wriggled uncomfortably, her eyes flitting about. "I don't have a lot of close friends."

"I don't think that's true."

"Not looking for sympathy. I have plenty of casual friendships, like with the women here, for example. But close girlfriends"—she shrugged—"not a lot. And then you and I hit it off ..."

"Over that perfectly rancid coffee."

"Right. You're the closest I've ever had to a sister."

"Aww."

Lily smiled. "And the last thing I wanted was for my dumb brother to mess that up for me!"

"Lily!" Addi smiled. "That would never happen."

"Yeah, I know." She shrugged. "But I got a little bossy, and I'm sorry."

"Forgiven. Of course. Nothing to forgive!"

"I've been thinking ... something about getting away from home and work makes that somehow easier." Lily looked fully at her now. "I would hate to think that fears are keeping you back from living your best life, Addi. I was serious when I said I prayed. And right now, my best advice to you is to put your life and your future in God's hands and see if he doesn't take you to greater places than you ever imagine!"

Addi grabbed her napkin and dabbed her eyes. "You're making me cry again!"

"Sorry."

She laughed lightly. "I'm so happy to have found a best friend in you too, Lily.

They rode back in silence mostly, not from tension, but each to her own thoughts. Lily pulled up to the curb near the Salvation Army drop off area, just east of Main Street.

"I'll help you." Addi popped open her door and stepped out. Fog had rolled in, giving the day a wistful look. Maybe later she would curl up on the couch with a blanket and read next to her fake fire.

Lily removed a bag from the back and sighed.

"It's hard, isn't it? To say goodbye to all the familiar things?"

"Yes. It truly is." Lily paused. "But at the same time, I'm happy that others will have some of Mom's lovely things to enjoy."

Lily handed her the bag, and Addi took two steps, her eyes brushing across the top of it. She stopped and set it down on the ground.

Lily pulled up behind her. "Was there something you wanted to keep? Sorry, I didn't ask you to look through things. I can be in a hurry sometimes. Feel free to do that before we donate, okay?"

Addi pulled a teddy bear from the bag and held it out to Lily. "Where ... where did you get this?"

"Oh that? Jax left it behind in his old room." She shrugged. "I thought he was a little too old to be playing with stuffed animals so—"

"It's mine. I mean, it's his. I mean ... I won this for him!"

"What in the world are you talking about?"

Addi clutched the animal. "This is the bear that broke up Jax and his fiancée."

Both of Lily's eyebrows shot up. "I have no idea what you're talking about, but, honey, if you want to keep it, it's yours."

Tears pushed forth from Addi's eyes. "I can't believe he kept it this whole time. When he told me about it, how Mara spotted it and Chase told her about me winning it,"—she held it out in front of her crying and laughing—"well, I figured she was long gone now."

Lily dipped her chin and stared. "Okay, so I thought I knew everything that was going on in my family, but you've got me stumped." She reached out and ran her fingers across the bear's head. "This is what ended Jax's engagement? A teddy bear that could frankly use a bath—and maybe some more stuffing?"

The memories of that night at the fair rushed back to Addi, the good ones, not the sad ones from the day after. She had kissed Jax that night. Only on the cheek, but he had looked at her fully for the first time in a year. She would never forget that, though she realized that she had repressed it for all this time.

"He whispered that he'd be back for me someday." Addi

sniffled and laughed. "He never said it would take twelve years!"

"I think I need to sit down."

"Oh, Lily. If the fire hadn't happened, and if I—we all—hadn't taken things into our own hands, life might look so different now."

Lily put the bag she was carrying on the ground and sat on a step. She pressed a hand to her cheek. "Have you been pining for my brother, really? All this time?"

"No." She hugged the bear to her chest. "But I wasn't moving forward with my life either."

Lily stood and put an arm on Addi's shoulder. "Well, girlfriend? Maybe it's time you did. God carries those burdens for us. You have no business trying to carry them around too."

Tears squeezed out of Addi's eyes and ran down her cheek. "I just hope it's not too late."

Chapter Eleven

"You have a conference call at nine a.m., a depo at ten, and a staff meeting at four." Tory paused. "You get all that, boss?"

Jax broke eye contact with the wall he'd been staring at, his voice distant, even to his own ears. "Call, depo, meeting. Sure."

Tory pushed off the doorjamb and over to the front of Jax's desk. "Maybe it's not my place to say this, but you look horrible."

Jax raised an eyebrow.

"I mean, you're still the young hotshot lawyer around here and all, but you need a haircut and maybe some sleep. You're kinda young to have such dark circles under your eyes."

"I'm not sure what to address first: the comments about my sleep and hair hygiene or your mention of that hotshot nonsense."

"Hey, I didn't say it"—Tory flapped the file in the air— "but the article in that legal journal did. So it's a cliché? I'm not the publisher."

"Will there be anything else?"

She stepped closer. "Seriously, have you been sleeping? Or maybe it's grief. You should probably see a counselor."

"Tory."

"Fine." She came around his desk with that file in her hands, then stopped to glance at the computer screen. "Looking for real estate?"

Jax scowled and reached for the computer mouse then shut down the screen.

"You think I'm nosy?"

He turned his chair so she would have to step back. "Did you say you had something else for me?"

"I do." She glanced at the file in her hands. "But if you're looking for property, you really need to call my friend Kim first. She's the best. I'll text you her digits, okay?"

Jax glared at his assistant. She had crossed the invisible line minutes ago and, typically, had managed to not only step on his last nerve but stomp all over it too.

She put on a smile. "Right. Okay. Here's the Stotland file. Ted Stotland would like to meet you for a drink tonight to discuss its contents. I told him you had a staff meeting at four, but he says he can wait. Shall I confirm?"

Jax stalled. That would mean leaving Olive alone far longer than he had planned today. Then again, it was customary at this firm to do whatever it took to secure files, even if that meant late nights that included expensive dinners and multiple bottles of wine.

Though he had happily participated in whatever it took on his way up the ladder, Jax's willingness to go to such lengths had waned recently. He flipped through his desk calendar, debating.

He snapped a look at Tory. "Tell him tonight won't work. However, I would be happy to arrange my schedule to meet him for coffee tomorrow morning." His tone told her this was not up for discussion.

Both of Tory's eyebrows shot up, and for once, she had no reply.

He continued, tapping his calendar. "I can do any time before ten a.m. Make sure to confirm the time for me before the end of the staff meeting."

"Absolutely." She placed the file on Jax's desk and left the office.

Jax watched her go, a rare sense of peace finding its way through him. Saying no was not as difficult as he thought it would be. Of course, he might have some explaining to do to his boss.

Jax paused and slowly opened his desk drawer, checking his phone. He had been back for nearly a month and still no word from Chase, though he had both texted and emailed him. That peace he had felt moments ago? It began dropping as quickly as a pelican after its prey.

He sat, working to center his mind, something he rarely had to do before he'd gone home to Saltwater. But that was before the revelations, before he had been confronted with the truth of the burden Chase had borne all these years—and his part in it. Over the past few weeks, the need to apologize in person to his brother had grown from a whisper to a clanging symbol. He would not rest completely until he could find Chase and apologize.

It remained to be seen whether that alone would bring Jax the sleep he so longed for.

Jax turned off his phone and shoved it back into his drawer, laying it next to his mother's Bible. With Lily's approval, he had carried it back from Saltwater with him. And he had been needling over a particular passage, one his mother had under-lined, ever since.

His mind rested on the problem of Chase, but what could be done about a man who didn't want to be found? Once again, the thought occurred that he could hire a private investi-gator. His firm had two on retainer, always at the ready to gather information needed to exonerate their clients.

But Chase owed him nothing, and smoking him out by heavy-handed means could have the opposite effect of causing him to retreat deeper into hiding. Jax stood and walked over to the window, taking in the energy of the city below him.

Later tonight, he would go home, put on his gym shoes, and take Olive for a long walk along the river. But now, he had work to do—and plenty of it. With a sigh, he opened the file she had left for him and began by examining the pleadings inside.

* * *

Hours later, Jax exited the conference room after finishing up his deposition. The court reporter just left, and he debated whether to go for a walk and pick up some coffee before the staff meeting later today. It would be warm, maybe even some-what humid, but he needed the break.

He ducked into his office to grab his wallet, with Tory on his heels. *Great.* The last thing he cared to hear right now was advice on what suburb would be best to invest in or what after-shave would make him smell better.

Jax swung around. "I'll be stepping out of the office for a short break. Can this wait?"

She frowned and shook her head. "I don't think so."

He swallowed a groan, keeping his expression neutral.

"It's just that, well, someone is here to see you, and it looks important." Tory leaned forward, lowering her voice into a conspiratorial whisper, that same one she liked to use whenever she had some delicious office gossip to serve him. "She says she has a family issue she needs to discuss with you."

Family issue. He sighed aloud this time. Jax's first six months as a lawyer were spent in a family law firm, and though the issues were important ones to tackle, he moved on quickly. He could not fathom spending his career watching couples fight over children or adult siblings squabble over their inheritance.

Tory continued, a goading tone to her voice. "I think the boss would like you to meet with this one."

Reality roared at him like a high-speed commuter train. Of course. He couldn't turn away someone only to have Patterson question him later. Resigned, Jax took a seat behind his desk. The walk would have to wait.

Tory disappeared, and a minute later, she entered and held the door open for a woman in a sundress and sandals.

His breath caught. "Addi?"

"It's me."

Tory backed out of the office, pulling the door with her. She slowed. "I will let Mr. Patterson know that you won't be able to make the staff meeting today because you are, uh, meeting with a client." She closed the door with a click, but not before sending Jax an over-exaggerated wink.

In two quick strides, Jax reached Addi. Instinct told him to wrap his arms around her and lift her above the ground. She wouldn't be able to run from him that way.

But he kept his exuberance in check, his mind ricocheting back to the last day they had seen each other in the hardware store. Addi had made it clear then that the possibility of them could never be. It sliced him up inside, and more than once he had to hold himself back from going over there one more time to plead his case. In the end, he showed her respect by accepting her decision.

But now?

"I've missed you." The words rolled from her beautiful mouth like a shy hush.

He took a step toward her. "You could've called."

Her lips dipped as if her resolve were being tested. Her eyes lowered, exposing a fluttering of dark eyelashes. "I suppose I could have. But ..."

She was an apparition, a mirage in his dry and thirsty life. No way could he be this blessed, this honored to have her here with him, not when he had let her down, had deserted their friendship so abruptly years ago.

When Addi raised her eyes to meet his, tears streamed from them. His throat clutched, emotion elbowing its way to the surface. She held up something in front of him. "You left this behind."

The bear.

Her eyes held a twinkle.

He cleared his throat. "I thought he might be more at home in Saltwater."

"Well, now, that might not have been the safest move 'cause I saved it from the giveaway pile."

He sucked in a breath.

She tilted her chin up, speaking lightly. "This bear has nine lives, apparently."

"Apparently so." He inched closer to her, closing the space between them a little bit more. "And so you decided that to keep him safe, you would bring him all the way out here to me."

"Well, I couldn't very well leave him there to be threatened by one of Lily's cleaning binges, now could I?"

"No, mm-mm, that would not be safe at all." He reached out and looped a stray tendril of hair behind her ear. Couldn't help himself. His voice had grown husky. Something else he could not seem to help. "Tell me why you're really here."

She shifted and gave him a little shrug. "I don't know what else to say, you big lug, except, I love you."

He tilted his head to the side, unable to tear his gaze from the sweet and shapely lips that had just uttered the words he longed to hear. Doing cartwheels in one's office was generally frowned upon at the firm, but who could blame him for wanting to?

Addi's eyes implored him. "Did you hear me?"

"I did."

"And?"

He could no longer contain his grin. Nor hold himself back from touching her skin. Jax took Addi's face in his hands and leaned his forehead against hers. "Coming from you, those are the most beautiful words I believe I've ever heard."

"Even the big lug part?"

"Especially that part."

He pressed his lips to her forehead, eyes closed, afraid to open them in case this was all his imagination. She sniffled, more proof that she really had come all this way, and he smiled. He walked over to the credenza, pulled a tissue from the silver-covered box, and handed it to her.

Addi dabbed her eyes, tears still streaming. "Thank you, but I think I'm going to need that whole box."

"It's yours." He leaned his bum against the desk and pulled her into his embrace. "Tell me everything. What changed your mind about me ... about us?"

She lifted her chin, her eyes searching his. "I— I never actually changed my mind. I was embarrassed, though, for living my adult life like some lovesick kid. When you yelled at me, I knew you were right—"

He waved his palms like windshield wipers. "I was not right."

"I thought I was doing the right thing, keeping Chase's secret, and I've already told you why. But I let it gnaw at me for years. As you know, I thought you were happily married with a dozen kids somewhere ..."

"A dozen?"

"Okay, a few." She exhaled. "But as you know, Chase filled me in on your breakup. Well, and then you gave me more than he did."

He had put his heart in his hands that day he went to the hardware store to reopen his past for Addi to see. Any hint he had made a mistake was gone now.

"Did you come here by yourself? How did you get here?"

"I flew. Teddy here helped me."

He pulled back. "Flew? You're kidding."

"You would prefer I took a Greyhound Bus?"

Jax laughed. "No. I'm just ... surprised."

Addi shrugged. "Guess when it matters, it's easier to bury your fears."

He grinned. "Is that right?"

"I just wish I could have been less afraid sooner."

"What have you been afraid of?"

"Of everything falling apart if I were to leave ... my mother's health, father's business, whatever."

"Maybe that's why you have compromised so much."

Addi nodded. "I really did want to follow you all to college."

"And that non-fireplace."

She paused, as if thinking about that. "It's cute, though. Don't you think?"

"Now that I think about it, yes, it's ... cute."

She laughed. "Boys don't like that word very much, do they?"

He tightened his hold on her.

"Seriously, though, for as long as I can remember, I've been making decisions as I go along in life. Never looking ahead or dreaming or making plans. Just living day to day."

"That's not so terrible."

"It is when you actually have dreams that you're ignoring." She paused and ran her tongue across her upper lip. "I've always believed in being other-centered, to take care of family."

"And that's what you've done."

"Yes, but for some reason, I've taken it on myself to fix everything that's broken around me—or at least, I've tried to."

"Like the situation with Chase. You kept his secret, even though it cost you something."

"I'm no hero, Jax. I knew your father would do right by mine, so I stayed out of it."

The rush of love he had for this woman had no bounds. "I need you to know something: my father knew. He knew that Chase had something to do with the fire, and he probably had a feeling that I wasn't innocent either."

"I don't understand."

"Addi, I learned recently that my father paid for the store's rebuild with his own money. Almost bankrupted him."

"But why? Is that the reason he sold the property so quickly afterward?"

"I believe so. From what I've been able to gather, he kept Chase and me out of trouble, though it cost him nearly everything. He sold the property to keep afloat, but unfortunately, the commercial real estate market was suffering from a downturn then."

"Oh, Jax. I'm sorry."

"I've thought so much about it the last few weeks. I was furious at first. My mother had to work after Dad died to keep money flowing in. If he had cashed in the insurance money, she could have had a nicer retirement to live on."

"But Chase—and by extension you ..."

"Yes. There would have been repercussions."

They were silent a moment. "But then your dear mother might not have enjoyed the love of so many animals."

He nodded, a smile turning up his mouth. "My mom always did find a way to make lack look like fun."

Addi exhaled a small laugh. "I can say the same for my mom. She's the reason I love to bake so much. Even when she was weak, she could sit in a chair and talk me through the next recipe."

"I wish I had spent more time talking to your mom, Addi."

"She always liked you, you know."

"Your mom had great taste."

Addi pressed the back of her hand to her mouth, stifling a smile.

"Seriously, though, I've never told you this, but I admired your dedication to your mom. As a kid, I'm not sure if I knew how to express that kind of appreciation, but looking back"—he choked up, surprising himself—"it taught me a lot."

"Yeah, Mama was worth it." Her eyes teared up again, and she slapped him on the lapel. "Stop making me cry so much already."

He caught one of her tears with his thumb, gently

sweeping it away. "Now that you've come to some conclusions about how you got here, what are you going to do about it?"

"I'll start by not enabling people."

"Your father, you mean."

"I can't blame him. Not really. I've been enabling him for years, but you know what? It served no good purpose to ignore his problems. I finally realized that. I think he did too."

"Ah, Addi." When it came to law, Jax often found the answers quickly. But love? That took time. "We're slow learners, you and me."

"Your sister said something similar to me. When I told her it was too late for you and me, she gave me that serious Lily-look of hers and said, 'Honey, it's never too late!'"

Jax chuckled. "Remind me to send that woman a bouquet of flowers tomorrow."

"My dad's realizing it's not too late for him either. Pastor Simon got to him. Dad's in drug and alcohol counseling now."

"That's amazing news. Does this mean you'll have to run the store, though?"

She pressed her lips together and shook her head. "I hired a manager for the store. Interviewed him myself and made sure he knew the difference between a flat-head screwdriver and a Phillips before I hired him."

"That's important." He paused. "So this means you have time on your hands then."

"Not exactly."

He raised a brow. The look she gave him nearly broke his heart. He brushed the back of his fingers down her cheek. "What is it?"

"Well, for starters, I've heard there are amazing gluten-free bakeries in Chicago, and I'd hate to come all this way and not visit each and every one of them."

"I agree. That would be a shame."

"I thought so."

"So do you mean to tell me that you came all the way here, on a plane—something you're terribly afraid of—for ... baked goods?"

Addi pulled her phone out of her purse and began typing on the screen. "Well, these bakeries have stunning reviews. You should see some of them."

Jax guided her phone down. "Addi."

She stared back at him, wide-eyed, a smile forming. "I also figured it would be one of the best ways to prove to you what I said earlier."

"That you love me." His voice had turned husky. This was not a question, because he knew by the way she looked at him now and how far she had come to tell him, that she loved him. But ... Jax would not mind hearing it from her lips again.

"Before you came back, Jax, I'd been looking for a way to move on, to stop living in the past, to finally break free from the worries and fears that seemed to have weighed me down. I was on my way."

"And then I showed up."

She grinned. "And then you showed up."

"Hmm."

"I do. Love you."

"And you proved it by flying all the way to Chicago."

She bit her lip, trying to tamp down the giddy smile on her face. No matter. The light in her eyes told him the truth. "Well, sure, that's one way to prove it to you, isn't it?"

"Uh-huh." He felt the warmth of her arms as they slid around his waist and tugged him closer.

"I do have something else to talk to you about, though—"

But Addi didn't have a chance to finish her sentence. Jax's

impatience had grown, and she was all too willing to table their discussion for another time, proven by the way she nestled into him. They swayed there intertwined, two hearts that had grown up together, finding safety in one another again.

She breathed a feathery sigh, and Jax tilted his head back to look at her. In her arms, he felt a purpose he had never known. He tipped her chin up, and with a quiet smile she flickered her gaze all over his face.

This is what he had wanted all along, to know that Addi wanted him as much as he did her. And by the way she clung to him as if she had no plans to let go now—or ever—he knew this would be forever. It just took them a little longer than most to get there.

Standing there, holding her, Jax marveled. She had flown all the way to Chicago, by herself, to tell him how she felt. He could not wait a second longer to show her how he felt too. Without a hint of doubt about Addison Marie Barrett's love for him, Jax lowered his lips to kiss her, the taste of her sweet, welcoming ... insistent.

* * *

"You're back."

Lily stared at them both, standing in the front foyer of the Cooper family home as Olive danced around her feet.

Jax stepped forward and swooped his sister in a hug. "Surprised?"

She smiled, looking from Jax to Addi and back again. She shook her head, bending down to pet Olive's head. "Not really."

Addi cracked up. "I twisted his arm and talked him into giving Saltwater another shot."

This time, Lily stood and her expression faltered. "Another shot? I don't understand. Jax? I thought you just accepted a partnership in Chicago."

He turned up his palms. "It wasn't the right move after all."

Lucky walked into the room just as Lily reached for a chair. "I think I need to sit down," she said.

"Jax? What're you doing back so soon? Hey, Addi." He looked from Jax to Addi, who beamed beside him. Olive bumped him with her head and brushed her coat with his hand. "You too, beautiful."

Jax took Addi's hand and kissed it. Lily gave them a little gagging sound, followed by a knowing laugh.

"Kind of a no brainer," Lucky said.

"Addi convinced me that my home is here, in Saltwater. With all of you." His voice broke on that last word.

"Whoa," Lucky said. "Didn't expect that though."

"Any word from Chase?" Jax asked.

Lucky frowned and shook his head. "Nothing."

Jax turned and caught eyes with Addi before continuing. "Okay. Well, we think we know where he is."

"Where?" Lucky asked.

"How?" Lily said.

Jax put his hand on Lucky's shoulder. "We're heading there now. Want to join us?"

"Hold on!" Lily shot up from her perch. "I want to come too. Oh, but wait. I have a Realtor coming this afternoon to list the house."

"Call her on the way." Jax opened the front door. "Tell her the listing's off."

Lily tilted her head aggressively, as if her brother had turned several shades of green. "And why's that?"

Addi stepped out of the door, followed by Lucky. Jax winked at Lily. "Because I've already found a buyer."

* * *

Pacific Coast Highway wound like a ribbon hugging the edge of the state. On one side, miles of mountains or sprawling land, and the other, blue stretching farther than the eye could see. They had been in the truck awhile now, their conversation no longer as animated as when they had first begun.

Addi stared out the window at the white-tipped waves. They passed Oil Piers Beach, her heart quickening, remembering Jax's stories of spending time with his father near there. It was late summer now, but beachcombers continued to fill the sand with their blankets and beach toys, as if unwilling to consider that fall would be coming soon.

She glanced behind her at Lily, whose eyes lolled against the truck's engine rhythm. Lucky seemed lost in thought, his own gaze focused out the window. Jax sat beside her, intent on keeping them safe on the road, but more than that, she suspected he was replaying words in his head that he would say once they found his brother.

If they found his brother.

Lily stirred and shot a look out the window. "We're almost there."

A sliver of worry turned over in Addi's heart. She hoped she wasn't wrong, but when she shared her epiphany of Chase's whereabouts with Jax, how he might have gone back to where his happiest memories had occurred, he agreed. Like Lucky said earlier, to them it was a no brainer.

Jax exited the highway and continued to drive the truck south on a frontage road that hugged the shoreline. Chase spent months out at sea for his work on ships, but he never tired of the ocean. Even when on dry land, he could often be found at the beach.

That's where he had found Addi after the fire, and it's the second main reason she thought to look for him here today.

Lucky strained his neck, searching for any sign of Chase. Jax was driving so slowly that several cars gunned passed him, one sending him an angry honk on his way by. Addi brushed her gaze at the man she openly adored. His teeth were clenched, so she touched his arm with her fingers. Noticeably, his jaw softened. He slid a look at her now; the warmth coming from him palatable.

"There!" Lucky said. "That's him!"

Campers and motorhomes parked bumper to bumper nearly filled Rincon Parkway, but each spot provided for one extra vehicle. Jax pulled into an open slot. Before he could shut off the engine, Lucky popped open his door and hopped out. Lily was close behind.

Jax cast a look at Addi. She slid over and kissed him on the cheek. "Commit your ways to the Lord," she said, reminding him of a verse they had both stumbled on recently. "I love you. It'll be just fine."

She watched as Jax hopped out of the truck and headed over to Chase, who had already been pulled into a group hug by the shoreline. The moment reminded her of a scene straight out of a movie drama with a beautiful ensemble cast. She debated. Would it be best to stay put? To give the family a chance to spend time alone in their tight circle?

As she stood marveling at forgiveness overflowing, Jax swiveled around. He grinned and waved her over to join them. From all appearances, the siblings looked like a happy family, but how would Chase feel about knowing she had given away his secret?

She swallowed back her nerves and exited the truck, the sun's rays warming her face. Jax pulled her close to him, which caught Chase's attention. The stubble he usually wore had turned into a beard during his time away, and his skin had become darker and red in places, but Chase's eyes were still as bright as ever. They alighted on Addi. Then on Jax. Then back to her.

"Whoa," he said, finally.

The siblings laughed in unison.

Chase continued to stare at Addi and Jax, the couple. He wagged his head. "Man. I leave for one minute ..."

"It was a lot longer than that!" Lily said.

Chase pressed his lips together, reminding Addi of Jax. He sighed, his shoulders settling, and put his hands on his hips. "I, uh ..."—he looked up—"I'm sorry. Needed some, uh, time to be alone with my thoughts. Lots to explain, I suppose."

Jax put a hand on his brother's shoulder, stilling him. "Understood. I have things to tell you too, but there'll be plenty of time to talk things out." He paused. "If you're ready to come back with us."

"Of course, he's coming back," Lucky said, making his way over to Chase's camper. He turned back. "Riding shotgun!"

Chase shrugged, both hands turned up. "The twin has spoken. So I guess that's that."

Epilogue

T hree months later

Jax stood inside the coffee shop watching the action. The place smelled of dark-roast beans from the richest soil. Lily appeared beside him wearing an apron that read *Sisters Coffee and GF Treats*.

"You ready to get out of here?" his sister asked him.

"Beyond ready."

Lily clucked a laugh. "Yeah, well, that's pretty obvious. You've been raking your hand through that hair of yours over and over."

"What's that supposed to mean?"

She poked her finger into his chest. "Means you're fixated on something."

Jax scoffed. His gaze traveled to the counter where Addi handed a customer a to-go bag.

Lily smirked. "Maybe I should have said on *someone*."

When they were still in Chicago those months ago, Addi told him that she had applied for a small business loan to purchase this place, but that she needed a cosigner. Without hesitation, Jax offered his signature. But to his surprise, she told him no. She wanted to ask Lily. So she did ... and the rest was history.

In that short amount of time, Jax had opened a small law practice in his hometown, gained a beloved wife, and watched her fulfill a lifelong dream. The speed of change in their lives had been dizzying, all-encompassing, but humbling and perfect, too.

Addi crossed the store and fell into Jax's arms. He kissed her as if they were the only two in the place. They had delayed their honeymoon until now, and he was beginning to show his impatience.

"Stop that." Lily whacked him with a set of tongs. "We have customers in here."

Speaking of which, Nate and Chase walked through the front door. Nate sidled up to the counter as Chase wended his way through the crowded store toward them.

Addi gave Jax a peck on the cheek. "I'll be back in a sec. I made Nate something special to try, and I need to grab it from the kitchen for him."

Reluctantly, he let her go.

"I'll follow you." Lily no doubt had become aware of the influx of new customers flooding through that squeaky-clean front door. Before she left, she said, "And don't worry about your Olive. Lucky's with her now, and I'll be watching after her for the duration of your trip!"

Jax smiled, grateful.

When Chase approached, he stuck out his hand, but Jax pulled him into a man hug, slapping him on the back.

Chase pulled away. "Pretty touchy-feely for a guy who used to be so formal."

"Guess you could say I'm a changed man." He gestured toward the one open table in the room. "Want to sit?"

"Only for a minute. Just came in for some of Lily's coffee. Can't get enough of the stuff."

They both looked at the front counter, where several people waited in line, then took a seat.

"You know," Chase said, "if the new office down the block doesn't work out, you could always hang a shingle out in front of this place."

"Work from here?"

"Yeah, like that show Ma and Dad watched when we were little." When Jax didn't respond, he went on. "It was called *Ed*? The guy called himself the bowling-alley lawyer?"

Dawning lit up in Jax's mind. "Righhhhht. So I'd be, what? The coffee shop lawyer?"

Chase clapped his hands and pointed. "That's it! Perfection, brother."

Jax laughed heartily.

Chase smiled mischievously. He dropped his gaze for a moment and brought it back up again. "Listen, I just wanted to say I'm glad about the way things turned out. You and Addi"—he shook his head—"as you know, I didn't see that one coming. I should have but didn't. I'm sorry for the hand I had in that."

"We've made amends, and I'll always be grateful for that. As far as I'm concerned, everything—all of it—is in the past now."

Chase nodded. "Excellent." His expression changed. "So ... Erica."

At the mention of Jax's new assistant, he frowned. "What about her?"

"I suppose she'll be holding down the fort while you and the missus are on your honeymoon. Okay if I check in on her?"

"Check in on her?"

He shrugged. "To see if she needs anything. She is new around here ..."

A slow smile came to Jax's face. He slapped his brother on the shoulder. "Yeah, uh-huh, you do that. Just don't scare her away—a good assistant is tough to find."

Chase stood and offered his brother a salute and a smile then ducked out of the coffee shop behind Nate.

Jax was still chuckling as Addi approached him. A smudge of flour—gluten-free, he assumed—streaked across her cheek. He gently wiped it away with his thumb. She caught his hand in hers and held it there, gazing up at him.

"Ready to go?" he asked.

The smile she gave him, so pure and full of love, told him, once again, he had made the right choice to move back to Saltwater Beach and restart his life here. Bonus: He had already set up his office right here on Main Street, where every day he would be working only a stone's throw from the love of his life.

His mother—and father—would be proud.

In answer to his question, Addi squeezed his hand and let out a tiny yelp. "Paris, here we come!"

Acknowledgments

If you've been a reader of mine for a while, you already know how much I love romance, ensemble casts, family sagas, and secrets that are carried for far too long. Hopefully *Reunion in Saltwater Beach* hits all those buttons—and a few more too.

As I was writing this story, life, as it sometimes does, took a sad turn. I want to offer deep gratitude to my editors who went beyond the call to help a girl out when she desperately needed the support. Many thanks to editors, Colleen Tomlinson and Jennifer Crosswhite.

Special thanks also to several longtime readers whose feedback helped me polish this story up to the *very last minute.* And to my daughter, Angie, for your extra help.

During writing season, my family gets to listen to me constantly say, "I'll do that after I finish this book ...!" So, thank you Dan and our kids—Matt, Angie, and Emma, and my mom, Elaine F. Navarro. Finally, a special whisper of gratitude and nod of love to my father, Dan Navarro, who passed away before publication.

* * *

And now these three remain: faith, hope and love. But the greatest of these is love.
- 1 Cor. 13:13

Free Ebook Offer

Join Julie's mailing list and you'll receive a free short e-novel
called *Dreaming of You.*
Sign up here:
www.juliecarobini.com/free-book

Also by Julie Carobini

This is Julie Carobini's complete library at the time of publication.

New!

Reunion in Saltwater Beach

Hollywood by the Sea Novels

Chasing Valentino (book 1)

Finding Stardust (book 2)

Sea Glass Inn Novels

Walking on Sea Glass (book 1)

Runaway Tide (book 2)

Windswept (book 3)

Beneath a Billion Stars (book 4)

Otter Bay Novels

Sweet Waters (book 1)

A Shore Thing (book 2)

Fade to Blue (book 3)

The Otter Bay Novel Collection (books 1-3)

The Chocolate Series

Chocolate Beach (book 1)

Truffles by the Sea (book 2)

Mocha Sunrise (book 3)

Cottage Grove Cozy Mysteries

About the Author

JULIE CAROBINI writes inspirational beach romances. She is the author of 22+ books across two names and is known for spunky heroines, charming heroes, quirky friends, and the secrets they keep. Her bestselling titles include *Walking on Sea Glass, Runaway Tide, Finding Stardust, The Christmas Thief*, and more. Julie has received awards for writing and editing from The National League of American Pen Women and ACFW, and she is a double finalist for the ACFW Carol Award. She lives on the California coast with her husband, Dan, and their rescue pup, Dancer.

Made in the USA
Columbia, SC
28 November 2022

72234744R00143